Welcome Home

or someplace like it

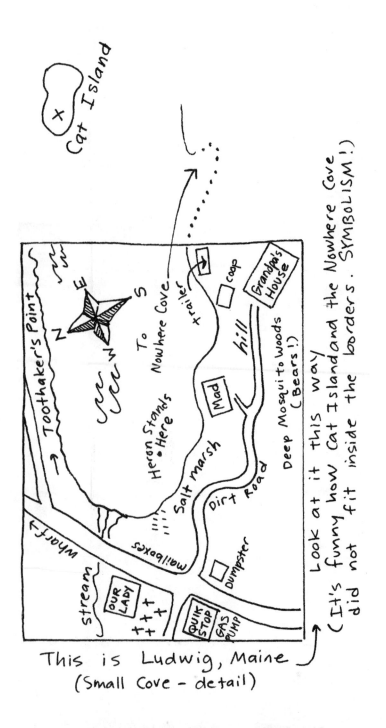

Cat Island

This is Ludwig, Maine
(Small Cove - detail)

Look at it this way/
(It's funny how Cat Island and the Nowhere Cove
did not fit inside the borders. SYMBOLISM!)

Welcome Home

or someplace like it

Charlotte Agell

Henry Holt and Company
New York

Henry Holt and Company, LLC
Publishers since 1866
115 West 18th Street
New York, New York 10011
www.henryholt.com

Library of Congress Cataloging-in-Publication Data
Agell, Charlotte.
Welcome home or someplace like it / written and illustrated by
Charlotte Agell.
p.   cm.
Summary: Thirteen-year-old Aggie Wing documents the events of her
summer in Ludwig, Maine, where she and her brother stay with their
ninety-one-year-old grandfather while their mother, a writer of
romance novels, is away doing research.
[1. Country life—Maine—Fiction.   2. Grandfathers—Fiction.
3. Friendship—Fiction.   4. Maine—Fiction.   5. Fathers—Fiction.
6. Diaries—Fiction.]   I. Title.
PZ7.A2665We 2003   [Fic]—dc21   2002038890

ISBN 0-8050-7083-4
First Edition—2003
Designed by Meredith Pratt

Printed in the United States of America on acid-free paper. ∞
10 9 8 7 6 5 4 3 2 1

To Peter, Anna, and Jon

Acknowledgments

Many thanks to Deb Dalfonso, Myrna Koonce, Karen Cook, and to my daughter, Anna Simmons, who read this book in its various stages and provided much insight and encouragement. I also appreciate the frank comments of many friends and relatives who read excerpts. To my editor, Christy Ottaviano, thanks for asking all the right questions. To my agent, Edite Kroll, I am most gratefully indebted.

Thanks also to Miriam and Erica Long for creative inspiration and to Monica Rose Henkel for knowing that Aggie's mother just had to be a romance writer, not an obscure poet. To my Communications students at the Harrison Middle School, much gratitude (and keep writing!). To Karen Guter, middle-school librarian extraordinaire, thank you!

Most of all, I would like to honor my husband, Peter Simmons, and my children, Anna and Jon, who lived with this book and me with great humor and confidence.

Welcome Home

or someplace like it

Anything can happen, anything is possible and likely.

—AUGUST STRINDBERG

June

June 3

It's morning again, a new gray day. Nothing's coming in on the radio but static. We've been driving since yesterday, which was about one hundred years ago.

"I don't think we're in Kansas anymore," says Thorne from the back seat, where he prefers to sprawl. Not that we've ever lived in Kansas, just a whole bunch of other places. Port Chester, New York, was where we just left. It was full of buildings and people. Here there are trees, trees, trees. I haven't seen a person for a mile and a half. Thorne's right, this definitely is not Port Chester.

We're headed down east, says my mother melodically. "Down east Maine, where the rising sun first kisses the shores of these United States." She's said that about ten times already, like some kind of radio jingle. She can be overly peppy when she wants us to like something.

"Uh-huh," I say, but I'm not really listening. I'm working in my notebook. It's notebook #27. The other twenty-six notebooks are in my duffel bag, which doesn't leave a whole lot of room for clothes. But that's okay, that's my history in there. I have notebooks going back as far as Omaha, and I was a really little kid when we lived in Omaha. If it weren't for the notebooks, I probably wouldn't remember much about life back then. (When I look at notebook #1, all the people in it are stick figures, and most of them have purple or green hair. Not to say anything bad about Nebraska. I liked it there.) Once in a while the car lurches and I mess up. Actually, this seems to be a particularly bad road for bumps.

"Mom," I groan, as if she's driving funny, which she isn't, even though she's been driving all night. She seems to get more careful the more tired she becomes.

I know it's just the road, but I like blaming her for stuff.

"Sorry, honey, frost heaves," says my mother, pushing her red hair out of her eyes. "I forgot about those."

I smile, thinking Honey Frost Heaves sounds like some indigestible cereal.

And suddenly our journey is over. Or at least we stop. We pull into Ludwig, population 159. It says so right on the sign. This is Ludwig: four corners with a church, a gas station, and a store called Ardis's Quikstop.

"But Ardis doesn't own it anymore," says Mom, who is an authority on Ludwig. She grew up in this town.

She gives a deep sigh and rolls down the window. We listen to the wind. She must hear me thinking too, because she says, "Don't worry, people live here. There *are* houses."

I don't doubt it, but I won't chime in all pleased. It wasn't my idea to come here, out to nowhere.

My mother gives another deep sigh and propels herself out of the car. It occurs to me that my life-of-the-party mom is actually nervous. Her short leather skirt looks kind of wrong next to all these pines.

Mom goes into the Quikstop and lets us both stay in the car.

"I want to say hello to Helen and Delwyn," she explains in a jittery way. "I haven't seen them in years."

And it is true. She's been gone from Ludwig forever. She's never taken us here, not once, and I'm thirteen. Thorne's almost sixteen. That's why he's not too thrilled. Coming way up here to Maine wasn't in his plans at all. Thorne was in a band back in Port Chester. Not that they were all that great.

Me, I don't plan much. So far I'm just along for the ride.

I look back at my notebook. Thorne's feigning sleep anyhow. I like that word: *feigning*. It's the noble way to fake it. My MOOSE CROSSING sign is too squiggly. Even with the car bumping all over the place, I should do better than that.

"Perseverance furthers," says Old Henry, the little Chinese man who lives in my pocket. He's pretty talkative for someone made of clay.

I pat my pocket and keep drawing. "Perseverance furthers." That's Chinese fortune-cookie speak for "keep trying." My new moose looks even worse, though. I'll have to find a REAL moose to draw. Should be easy, judging from all the MOOSE CROSSING signs we've gone by.

I got Old Henry when we lived in Hawaii, back in the days of Dad. Hawaii is also where I saw my favorite road sign, TURN ON HEADLIGHTS IN CLOUDS, a very useful

the
↓ sea

Where is this road taking us?

thing to do up on Haleakala, the old volcano. I could fill half a notebook with the funny road signs I've seen.

My last picture of Dad is back in notebook #8. According to that picture, he was about nine feet tall (or I was a bug) . . . the biggest man on earth. From what's left of him in the few photos we have, I don't think he was actually that large. It's hard to tell. Mom was so mad at him that she snipped him out of everything. Dad disappeared after we left Hawaii for Cincinnati. Thorne says Dad went out for a can of Campbell's Tomato Rice soup and he never came back. I don't know why he left, but every time I eat Campbell's Tomato Rice soup, I feel forlorn, which is a pretty good word for a bad feeling.

Thorne and I argue about Dad a fair amount. We're good at arguing. Like I think Dad had a mustache, but Thorne

scissors are hard to draw

What kind of mustache?
a) b) c) none

Where my dad used to be
there is a hole.

says no. Just because he's older, he thinks he's always right.

We've asked Mom about the mustache and a lot of other things. Her answer is always the same: "That man? Don't even bother."

Since she doesn't feel like talking about it, Thorne and I make up stories about him.

I say he's the captain of a ship that sails the China Sea.

Thorne laughs at me and says I have a Pippi Long-stocking complex. It's true that I used to LOVE Pippi. And her father was a captain in the South Seas, but nobody believed her until he showed up one fine day! Thorne has far less imagination. He claims Dad is a toll collector in Arkansas.

I tell Thorne he doesn't even know if there ARE tolls in Arkansas.

"Sure there are," he says, although it's not one of the places we have ever lived. Neither is China. But mustache or no mustache, I still remember him kissing me with tickles.

Our mother is taking her sweet time. I sit there reading the signs in front of Ardis's Quikstop. Sullenly is how I sit, just in case anyone is watching me. The signs are pretty strange:

VIDEO RENTALS

NIGHT CRAWLERS

TAXIDERMY BY DELWYN

"Hey, Thorne," I say, poking at him. "What do you suppose night crawlers are?"

"Worms," he says. "For fishing." He shrugs, like knowing everything in the world gets to him. He drapes his long legs over the top of the driver's seat. Thorne's tall and skinny, just like me. He's a geeky-looking kid with a striped wool cap pulled low over his eyes. Maybe he doesn't need them to see; maybe he navigates by echolocation or something. That's what bats do, and they prefer the night to the day too. Thorne's a freak.

He doesn't want to talk, but I keep after him. "And what's taxidermy again?" (As if I ever knew.)

"It's when you stuff dead animals."

"Oh." This sounds like a pretty thrilling town. "I wonder if they stuff moose?"

"Shut up," Thorne says. I know he thinks I'm being like Mom, Overly Cheerful. But really I just want to know stuff.

Like what in the world are we doing up here?

I suppose I should feel excited about meeting Grandpa. It's his house we are going to. We'll be staying in my mom's ancestral homestead and everything, probably for the whole summer.

I guess Thorne's just being more honest, plastered to the back seat with his eyes closed. Dreaming of elsewhere.

I pull Old Henry out of my pocket and look at him. He's intact, considering all the pockets he's lived in (all mine . . . I just keep growing). He looks fairly dignified for someone with lint all over his head. I flick it off. He winks at me.

"Someday I'll get you more elegant accommodations," I whisper, and stuff him safely back into the pocket of my soon-to-be-way-too-small favorite overalls.

A car pulls into the lot and a lady inside looks at me with distinct curiosity. Maybe they don't get too many strangers up here. I feel like a coming attraction. I smile a limp smile and think about waving, but I figure she'll get the whole story when she goes inside for milk and finds my mother there: Meredith Bellicose, home at last.

I wait an eternity. Mom doesn't come out. I guess it's not a Quikstop after all (ha ha). Thorne is now really asleep. In fact, he's snoring. How charming.

It's not hot out, but the inside of the car feels clammy. I decide to investigate. For a terminally shy kid, I'm pretty brave around strangers. I get out of the car. My legs feel stiff from sitting still for so long. I wonder how I look.

In the side-view mirror I see a skinny girl who definitely needs her bangs cut. I have blackheads on my chin. My eyes are gray at the moment, although sometimes they turn green. They are definitely my best feature. My mom's latest ex-boyfriend, Ricky the Landscaper-Bodybuilder-Dude, used to say that I had "faraway eyes." I didn't much like Ricky, but I think he was right about my eyes.

Me!
(in Ludwig, Maine)

    I gear up to go in. This is not an elegant place. Last year's leaves are still stuck in the grates of the stairs. There isn't anything in the way of landscaping, unless you count that field of ferns unfurling greenly across the street by the church. I guess Ricky taught me to look for landscaping. But this place is wild.

Even the church is called Our Lady of the Wilderness. It has a scraggly looking cemetery, a tall white steeple, and pointy stained-glass windows. It's a pretty little church. "So New England" is what Tour Guide Mom would say.

I push open the door to Ardis's Quikstop. This place is messier than any room I've ever lived in, and believe me, I don't care about folded clothes. (That's Thorne. He's the neatnik kid, although you might not guess that by looking at him.) Every square inch of Ardis's is COVERED IN STUFF. Cereal boxes, six-packs of beer. Carpet cleaner. Lots of caps, but only in orange. Orange must be really "in" up here. Soap bubbles. Beanie Babies. Cans and cans of soup, including, yes, Campbell's Tomato Rice. I reach out and hold a can, just for a moment.

Somewhere there is a TV on. I make my way around the aisle, past that lady I saw outside. She smiles at me again, and I nod. She has a beautiful, long gray-brown braid, kind of like someone from a fairy tale. She's wearing overalls too, all covered in paint splats. That's how I want to look when I grow up. I blush and stare down at the scuffed-up linoleum. My thoughts seem so public sometimes.

I find my mom sitting at sort of a mini-diner, kind of like the one back in Port Chester. She's perched on one

Melancholy

There is nothing sad about soup.

of those spin-around stools with the red fake leather tops and the faux-silver bottoms. That's another good word for fake: *faux*. It's French.

Scrutiny. It sounds painful, and it is. Three faces look at me. My mother's and the people I know must be Helen and Delwyn. Helen stands behind the pink slabs of dead animal, a cleaver comfortably in her hand. A sign behind her proclaims BEST BACON IN LUDWIG. I'll bet anything that it's the ONLY bacon too. Delwyn is this mousy little man who probably doesn't argue much with Helen. I wouldn't if I were him. Helen looks kind, but I always feel sort of nervous around people in hair nets. It must be Lunch Lady Phobia, which I developed from the especially mean ones in New Jersey and Detroit. (I have six I HATE HER pictures of the lunch lady with the maroon hair in notebook #18. She was particularly bad.)

"Honey," says my mother, "meet Helen and Delwyn. Helen and Del, this is my baby, Aggie." I grin at them, politely ignoring the fact that my mother just called me baby.

"Pleased to meet you," says Delwyn, giving a sort of bow. He's just this little dab of a man. He kind of reminds me of Old Henry with the bowing and everything.

"You look like your poor dead grandmother," Helen says cheerfully. Her upper arms wobble. She and Delwyn make me think of Jack Spratt and his wife. The back of my mind starts singing:

> *Jack Spratt could eat no fat.*
> *His wife could eat no lean . . .*

I nod at Helen, but I'm a little confused. I don't even know my grandmother's name. My mother hasn't seemed that into family before now. When she first brought up our trip to Maine, she just said there were some of our people here. People. As if we were part of some nameless tribe.

It seems like Mom could stay in the Quikstop for hours, but finally we say good-bye to Helen and Delwyn and get back into the car. Thorne is still asleep. I guess he doesn't care about grand entrances. He's had so many new lives that one more isn't going to make him sit up and take notice.

Mom's talking about my grandfather as if she were describing a character in one of her books. Mom writes what Thorne calls "bodice rippers." That's because the covers of her books have people kissing on them—most romance books do—and the women almost always have skimpy, unlaced tops. Even the titles are like that: *Sweet September Embrace* or her latest, *Almost Amber*. Sappy, sappy, sappy! She's kind of famous, actually, if you like that sort of thing. Which I DON'T! Mom talks about life as if it were a kind of book we were living. We are the word people, Thorne and Mom and I, although we hardly ever seem to REALLY talk.

"Grandpa has lived alone for years," says my mother. "His wife left him for the big city, where they say she spent her declining years pushing a shopping cart of returnable bottles up and down the main drag." Mom's smoking a cigarette while she's telling me this, a thing she does when she gets jumpy.

"You mean Grandma was a bag lady?" I ask.

"Not Grandma, honey. His second wife, Eileen. Mom died before you were born. You know that."

And I do, kind of. It's all pretty vague, because I never actually met any of these strangers, my family.

"Emphysema," I say, nodding. "Grandma died of emphysema." For a long time, I didn't know what that word meant, but now I do: death by smoking. Mom should take a hint, but instead, she just takes another drag.

"Grandpa didn't marry Eileen until I was already gone. He sent me pictures, though. I always hoped it would last, since I didn't want to think of my father all alone in that big house. Before I could get around to meeting her, she had moved out."

I try to imagine my grandfather. I know he's old. *Really* old. He was almost sixty when my mom was born. I try to imagine Mom out here in the country, growing up with her old dad. But I can't picture it. Mom's so *city*.

I can't even stay in my seat belt, I'm *that* excited. I poke at Thorne. I swear his hat looks like a tea cozy. A teeny ponytail sticks out of the tea spout hole. I give it a little tug.

I wonder what this grandpa of ours will make of Thorne. My brother's kind of unusual. He collects paper clips and talks in his sleep. Like right now he's mumbling "breath mints" over and over. Weird. Thorne doesn't even wake up as we bounce the last half mile to the house on a dirt road full of potholes.

"Small Cove," announces our mother, and I think she is making a geographic pronouncement. Because that is what I see before us. The road has twisted and turned and left us here by the choppy sea. There is a small house and a rather large one, perched dangerously near a cliff. But it turns out that Small Cove is the name of where we are and where Mom grew up, and I see that her eyes are welling with tears. Her mascara is running. She blinks.

"Grandpa is expecting us," she says, and already I know that word travels fast out here. Thorne stirs as we bump the final few yards to the house by the edge of the cliff. It's huge and begging for paint. Scraggly beach roses bloom by the door. There's a strange little room on top.

Mom pulls over next to an abandoned chicken coop, which tilts away from the sea, gray and windblown.

"Did you know I kept chickens when I was a kid?" she tells us.

And that just strikes me as the funniest thing. I mean, MY mother—with her nail polish and jewelry—a keeper of chickens?

Slowly we unfold ourselves from the car, leaving our luggage behind for now. We walk solemnly up to the front door. A procession of three.

Mom knocks. We stand there, observed by some circling gulls and a rather opinionated crow in a tree.

And Grandpa.

If there were curtains in the windows, one would have been pulled aside for the eye of Grandpa, because, suddenly, I feel it upon us.

We wait.

My Mom— now does SHE look like a chicken expert?

We wait and wait.

Just as our mother is about to walk right in to what was, after all, her home once upon a time, we hear steps. Someone is dragging his legs to the door, and it opens. There is Grandpa. Eugene Bellicose is his name. I can tell at once that he's been a sea captain, a real captain. His face looks so old. His eyes are yellow. If mine are faraway eyes, his win the distance award.

"Dad," says Mom, leaning forward. Her wild, not-at-all-limp-like-mine hair glints in the sun, and she looks like a movie star from some old-timey movie. Grandpa just stands there and doesn't reach out for her. He's staring at Mom, staring at us. Finally, his lips move a little, like a smile or a word might possibly embark from them, and the door opens a bit wider. "Come in," this means. I just know it does.

So we enter. Immediately, there is a cat by my shins, arcing its back like a dolphin. . . . I smile and bend over. This is my welcoming committee.

"Oliver," speaks our grandfather, and I guess he means the cat.

We follow him down a long hall to the kitchen. The floorboards squeak in agony. It's *so* warm in the kitchen with the sun pouring in and a strong fire going in the world's biggest woodstove. A kettle is beginning to whistle. There is the stuffy smell of old person. But all this is hard to take in, because we are distracted by the most monumental greeting: a four-layer cake. It sits regally on the table. Frosted, all cream and sugar, anointed with wilting violets.

"You can eat those, you know," says Grandpa, pointing at the violets. His voice seems to have warmed up a little. Maybe he doesn't use it much. The cream on the cake has gone as yellow as the whites of his eyes. It doesn't seem all that fresh. I think maybe Grandpa has been expecting us for days, if not years.

"Why, Dad!" exclaims Mom in her theatrical voice. "It's beautiful."

"I baked it myself," says Grandpa, and beams like the world's oldest lighthouse. I lean over to check out the violets. I try not to breathe, because, truly, that cream must be rancid. Poor Thorne, I think, and I see him turning pale. We haven't had any breakfast, and Thorne doesn't do dairy to begin with. I peer at the cake and see little cat licks and a place where a thumb might have been. Still, it's impressive in an architectural sort of way.

The problem is—Grandpa wants us to eat it.

He moves to the stove and pours hot water into a blue china teapot. He motions to the table. "Sit down."

Cutting the cake is like slicing into a mountain. I can feel the three of us holding our breath, waiting for the whole thing to topple.

But Grandpa is a cake magician, and he carves out five equal and enormous slices. His plates are covered with ornate blossoms and cracks. Grandpa leans over, slowly, slowly, and puts one of the plates on the floor. Oliver comes over to sniff it.

"Sometimes he eats at the table," says Grandpa. "But I push him off."

We all sit there together. If I don't breathe through my nose, I can choke down some bites. I slosh it down with tea so hot it scalds my throat.

"So . . . ," says Mom, but nothing more comes out because Thorne runs from the table and down the squeaky hall. Through the smeary window I can see him retching into the roses. He does not return.

"Why won't he take off his hat?" is all Grandpa says, and I start to worry how our little visit will end up. I am the best one at worrying in our family. "Why waste such a talent?" Ricky the Landscaper-Bodybuilder-Dude used to tease me, but I would just roll my faraway eyes.

The minutes pass like hours. I sit there politely, drinking the tea as it cools. I've probably had five cups by now. There's still a lot of cake on my plate. After hearing Thorne throwing up, I just can't eat any more.

Finally, Grandpa gets up in very slow motion and shuffles over to an old rocker by the woodstove. He sinks down into it with relief printed all over his face. His eyes close. Maybe it is time for his nap. Maybe we are too much for him. I pat Oliver. He's gray with white speckles and purrs like a motorboat. So far he's what's best about Small Cove.

"We have to remember, he's ninety-one years old," says my mother, referring to my grandfather as if he weren't really there.

She goes out to get our stuff and check on Thorne. I should stand up and help her, but this is one warm cozy cat and I just don't feel like moving.

Thorne

June 4

My first morning in Small Cove, I run down to the sea. The tide is in, and the waves are wild. I want to go swimming.

"It's too cold, honey," says Mom.

"You're crazy," adds Thorne.

"Let her go," declares my grandpa, and I figure he's the boss.

I'm wearing last year's swimsuit, which is killing me. How could I ever have wanted anything this pink? Besides, it's way too small. I must have grown three inches. I let the straps slide off my shoulders. Nobody's watching anyway. I'm dying to swim. I LOVE swimming. It's one of the things I am actually good at. Thorne says it's because I have big feet, but I think he's just jealous. I can beat him in a race, any stroke, any day! (And his feet are bigger, so there!)

I stick my toe into the gray-green waves.

It turns into an ice cube in three seconds flat.

I stand there in the wind, stalling. By now my teeth are chattering. I tell the gulls, "I . . . I j-j-just wa-want t-t-t-to go SWIMMING!"

I'm not the sort of person who likes to give up once I have an idea, so I decide to count to three and then jump in. I get to eight and decide if I don't go by ten, I'm a complete and utter failure.

TEN! I fling myself in. I'm running in knee-deep ice-cold water on really sharp rocks and seaweed, but that does the trick. I slip and fall headlong into the waves.

And swim!

It's not so bad once I'm totally numb.

I don't stay in all that long, that's for sure. I guess the Gulf of Maine is just chillier than anyplace I've ever been swimming before.

Stiff with cold, I clunk into the kitchen.

I make it over to the roaring woodstove and drip on it. Each drop sizzles and dances and is gone. Grandpa hands me a mug of hot tea with just the right amount of milk. He asks if I want sardines on toast, and I say yes, even though you have to eat them bones and all.

I think I will swim every day I am here.

① Stick one toe in. Pull it out.

② Count to three.

③ Fail to jump in.

④ Count to 10, very slowly. Twice.

⑤ When you get to 11, Scream LOUDLY and jump in no matter what!

Laughing Gull

How to Get in the Water in Maine (serious applicants only)-this works!

June 9

We've been here for almost a week. The bell buoy keeps me awake at night. The bell buoy is this big, clanging thing out in the bay. Otherwise, I'm actually getting used to being here. It's sort of like a vacation in the clouds, all wind and moisture. It's funny about the bell buoy keeping me up, though. Our apartment in Port Chester was downtown, and the nights were totally noisy with cars and sirens and people yelling. I slept right through all that. It's the quiet that gets me. The bell buoy is just like punctuation; it points out the endless silence and makes you hear it even more.

We haven't seen much of Thorne. He does seem to have recovered from the cake incident with enough dignity to manage coming down for supper. All the meals so far, after the cake that is, have been some kind of fish: poached whitish fish, boiled even whiter fish, fried some-kind-of fish. It's not bad really. Plus Mom and Grandpa have been cooking together, and they are entertaining to watch. They're like a bizarre cooking show on TV: *The Movie Star and the Geezer Seafood Show.* They don't talk much, and their conversations seem to be in some kind of code:

"Weren't much pep in Delwyn when he was a younger man."

"Nope. Not hardly."

"But then a person can surprise you."

"Yup." Long pause. "Yup."

And that's my mother saying the nope-not-hardly and yup stuff. She's drifting back into some kind of accent thing, and it's very funny.

I walk around copying her, sucking in air as I say "Ayuh, ayuh, ayuh," until she swats me with the dish towel. She seems to be in a good mood, and pretty soon I find out why.

"How would you feel if I left you two with Grandpa for a little while?" She asks me this as the two of us are washing dishes in Grandpa's huge slate sink. "Just while I go to Niagara Falls for a few weeks."

"Niagara Falls, the honeymoon spot?" I ask. "Why Niagara Falls?"

I know the answer before she says it.

"Book research."

It seems my mom can't write one of her books without going on what she calls "location." Personally, I think Small Cove would make a great place for a love story. There could be kissing by the moonlit cove or something.

I hunch my shoulders and keep scrubbing away at the fishy frying pan. Oliver is walking back and forth between my legs, rubbing himself all over me and purring. I think he loves me, or maybe it's the fish scraps he's after.

"Sure. Go ahead," I say, but that doesn't mean I'm glad about it.

"Thanks, honey."

Maybe I give her writer's block or something, and *that's* why she always has to leave.

"Oh great," says Thorne when I tell him. "She'll take the car, and we'll be marooned up here."

It's not like he drives or anything, but I know what he means.

Mom makes me give him the news, which isn't so very brave of her. She's down at the Quikstop, probably telling Delwyn and Helen to keep an eye out for us. Not that we aren't used to this Mom-leaving-us-for-a-few-weeks thing.

She's left us a lot. She left us in Dayton, Denver, and Detroit. She left us in Tucson and Teaneck. I make it sound like a song, but it's true. Except that we never did live in Tucson, I just needed another *T* town. Anyway, if we had lived in Tucson, she would have left us there too.

Unlike Dad, she always *does* come back.

When we were little she wouldn't be gone so long, just a few days here and there. Usually she'd ask some old lady with a foreign accent to watch us. I remember one called Minette and one called Irish Hester and one who insisted on Mrs. Steppinski. There seem to be lots of unemployed old ladies with foreign accents all over this country, just waiting around to watch the neighbor's children for a week. For a couple of summers we got to go to camp. Mine was called Minnetonka and was somewhere in upstate New York. I found fossils and animal bones. That's where I became practically an Olympic swimmer.

In Port Chester she left us all by ourselves, but it wasn't so bad because Thorne did all the grocery shopping and cooking, and he's actually the best cook I know. Maybe when Mom leaves I'll ask him to whip up some of his special pasta sauce for Grandpa and us. With linguini, if they have that up here.

"Just go," we tell her, because at this point, that's what she's going to do anyhow.

June 10

And go she does.

"Bye!" She waves jauntily from the old Honda. Her lipstick matches her car: RED.

Thorne and I wave, but we don't smile. We have to punish her, just a little. I can hear the growl of the car engine long after Mom's disappeared from sight.

So now it's just Thorne and me and Grandpa and Oliver the cat. And Old Henry. I always have Old Henry. I take him out of my pocket and hold him to my cheek.

I blink and remember my father. He's the one who gave me Old Henry in the first place. Sometimes I think that my real dad knew he was going to get lost and never come back again, so he left me another guy, an old Chinese dad with a very bad sense of humor. I kiss him and put him back in my pocket. It makes me feel better every time.

Oliver is the most energetic of the bunch of us. Grandpa naps, Thorne sulks, and I walk around wondering what to do. Oliver and I pal around. He has shown me the entire house from a cat's-eye view. There are two staircases, five bedrooms, and only one bathroom. There is an armchair, quite excellent for sharpening your claws. But the best part is that strange room at the top of the

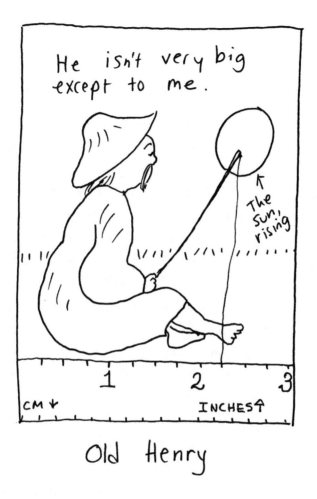

He isn't very big
except to me.

The sun, rising

1   2   3
CM↓   INCHES↑

Old Henry

house, which is called a cupola. (Grandpa told me that,
not Oliver.)

The cupola is a wide-open place, good for watching
sunrises in case you wake up too early. Which I do. It's a
drafty little room for pacing around, worrying. Grandpa
calls it the widow's walk. This is where the captain's wife
would sit, looking out to sea, waiting for her husband.
Maybe there has been some worrying done in this room

before, although Grandpa doesn't get too specific about Grandma.

Still, I think *every* house should have a cupola, like a refined corner of the mind. This is the perfect place to sit and work in my notebook. This is the perfect place to walk around thinking about my mother. Meredith Bellicose.

Or I *should* say, Cassandra Laurence. That's her pseudonym. That's what it says on all her books. Cassandra Laurence just *sounds* more like a romance writer than Meredith Bellicose. Meredith Bellicose sounds like she should write law texts or something. I like pseudonyms. There's Mark Twain, who was really Samuel Clemens and found his new name when he worked on a riverboat. And Lewis Carroll, who was really Charles Lutwidge Dodgson, a mathematician. Or Lemony Snicket, who has just the best pseudonym of all! (It sounds like some kind of grumpy pastry.)

Now, I'm someone who really could use a pseudonym. Take my real name, for example: Aggie Wing. Agatha. Who would name a baby that and *why*? It sounds like a name that ought to be reserved for eighty-year-old women. Crabby women. Anyhow, my parents somehow didn't realize this. I have thought of about a million pseudonyms over the years. My notebooks are full of them. But they never seem to stick. Way back in notebook #2 there is Lucy Apple. I used to just LOVE the name Lucy, and apples are still my favorite fruit. Boring but true.

Some of my own past pseudonyms are:

Brittany M. Unicorn (you can tell I was nine at the time!)
André Lucide (from my French period)
Orla Drybeck (just plain weird!)
Spectra Blue (I'm fond of that one, since it came off a paint chip. We were painting our apartment. This was back in Teaneck, New Jersey. As I recall, we only stayed there about five months, but the act of painting the apartment gave me great hope, like we were actually committing to something. Mom and Thorne chose color names too. I still remember them: Heather Pink and Hunter Green. For a while we even called each other Heather, Hunter, and Spectra Blue. But it didn't last, and neither did New Jersey.)

All my pseudonyms wear off. So for now I'm Aggie. Aggie Bellicose Wing. At least my last name's good. I've been thinking I could go by just my last name, like a rock star. WING! (And if I ever marry anyone named Prayer, we could be a Wing and a Prayer, which means something, but I'm not sure what.)

There was a girl I knew back in Detroit, Isla Fire. (Talk about a cool name! Or actually a hot name, practically volcanic!) She taught me this formula for a pseudonym: You use your middle name and the street you live on. But that would be a DISASTER for me. Just imagine it. My middle name is BELLICOSE, meaning argumentative (that's nice!), and I don't even know if this place HAS a street name. FIRE LANE 23, or something, is what it says up by the road.

Bellicose Fire Lane 23.
No thank you.

A complete list of books by Cassandra Laurence, aka Meredith Bellicose:

Sweet September Embrace
The Hour of Fire
Passion in Pittsburgh
The Betrayal of Blair
Midnight's Agony
Toward Morning Together
Heather in Bloom
Almost Amber

Mom's pretty prolific, which means she writes a lot. That's not to say it's any good. Just listen to the blurb on the *Midnight* book:

> *Elspeth McGuire, a beautiful young governess, loses her way one dark night. She is taken in by Roy, a handsome, mysterious stranger. Together they discover what fires burn in the night. Sorrow, however, is looking over Elspeth's shoulder.*

I mean, give me a break. This is the same mom who tells me not to have anything to do with strangers. And who's Sorrow? The dog?

"It pays the bills" is what Thorne says. He's just not as critical, I guess.

One of Mom's book covers— sappy, sappy, sappy!

June 13

Thorne makes himself scarce. From what I can tell, he's going to spend the summer lying on his bed with his headphones listening to that German techno-pop he likes. Not the most social way to be. He hasn't even offered to make his famous pasta sauce yet. So Grandpa feeds us, or we walk up to the Quikstop to buy these huge submarine sandwiches that we're supposed to call "Italians." You pronounce it "Eye-talian." Don't ask me why. Helen and Delwyn are very friendly. I can sit on one of their diner stools and spin half the morning away. They have this drink called Moxie, which sort of tastes like fizzy cough medicine, but other than that it's really good. All kinds of people come to the Quikstop. Well, maybe at least seven or nine a morning. Like that woman with the braid. It turns out that her name is Haley WING, which is an amazing coincidence. But as far as I know, Dad wasn't from around here. Idaho, I always thought. Other than that, it does seem like everyone is related around here. Mom never took Dad's name. She kept Bellicose, even though she's not particularly argumentative. Wing might suit her better, since she's always flying the coop. Wing certainly suited Dad.

Anyway, this Haley Wing person is an *artist*, and to me that's just the best fabulous omen. One of these days I might even open my mouth and talk to her.

Delwyn and Helen keep asking me if I've met Mad yet, and I say, "No, I haven't." They say, "Well, yah, she's so busy this time of year, with school and softball and clamming." And I don't ask any questions, because I don't want to seem too uncool, and besides, Mom took Thorne and me out of school way too early this year and I'm annoyed to even talk about it. Anyhow, apparently Mad's my neighbor and also my age. So I'm keeping my eye out. Meanwhile I'm watching people come and go. So far Ludwig seems to mostly consist of a bunch of old men who play cribbage. "The boys," Delwyn calls them, although the youngest one must be at least seventy years old.

When I'm not at the Quikstop, I'm sitting up in the cupola, scanning the horizon and the entire cove for this Mad person. I'm hardly used to such a quiet life. In Port Chester we at least had the mall. (I don't like malls, but it *was* someplace to go.) In Port Chester we at least had TV. (I don't like TV, but it *was* something to watch.) Up here the wind blows, and the seagulls call. Once in a while the old crow caws from the dead tree. It's like a poem about nothing at all.

So that's why I look for Mad. She's got to be more interesting than Thorne, that slug. (Not that I'm desperate, but I am.)

Helen at the Meat Counter

June 17

Grandpa does his best to keep me busy. He goes down to the landing just about every day for bucket loads of fish for our all-fish diet. He's taught me how to gut a herring. What you do is cut its head off and then slit its belly with a knife. Grandpa even gave me a knife. He says it was my mom's when she was little. If I'd had a knife this cool, I wouldn't have just left it here!

For some reason, I don't mind cutting up fish. The best part is, when you're done you go out and stand on the edge of the cliff, throwing the bucket of guts up into the air piece by piece. Out of nowhere, a gull will swoop in and catch the treat midair. Then two gulls come, then seven, and then so many that the sky is just shrieking. Fish guts get on my hands, but I don't care. I am Aggie, fishergirl.

Anyway, it beats moping in my room like Thorne. I invited him to fling fish guts, but he just mumbled something. From the smell of the hall outside his room, he's taken up smoking again. The only mystery is: How's he getting the cigarettes? The sign at the Quikstop plainly says you have to be eighteen. And Thorne does NOT look eighteen, no matter what he thinks.

My room is right next to Thorne's. It has yellow wall-paper and a white cast-iron bed. I pretend to be the heroine in a book. Not my mother's kind of book. A book from long ago, like maybe by Dickens. In fact, there are plenty of books in my room. Most of them are too young for me, like *Black Beauty*. But that's okay. I'll read them again. I'll read just about anything. My eyes fly to words like moths come to Grandpa's backdoor light. Shampoo labels, cereal boxes, nutrient information about Moxie (twenty-five grams of sugar)—I read them all.

Grandpa reads too.

He sits by the woodstove and reads the obituaries in the newspaper.

"See, Death's the next trip I'm taking," he tells me, without batting an eye. "And I'd just like to know who has gone there first."

For a ninety-one-year-old, Grandpa's pretty energetic. But he still needs to take about three naps a day. Maybe that's because he hardly sleeps at night. I'm not the best at it either. I came down after midnight for a glass of milk, and there he was, doing a gigantic jigsaw puzzle, the thousand-piece kind. It was a puzzle of a clipper ship. I helped him with a tiny bit of the rigging.

"Ever climb up in one of those?" I ask him.

"Just how old do you think I am, young lady?" he says. And I guess that means no.

He has many more wrinkles. His face looks like leather. His eyeballs are all yellow from all his time at sea. Under his cap, he is bald.

Grandpa

June 19

Mom's been gone for a week and a half. It seems like longer. Almost every night she calls us from Niagara Falls. The first time I was a little disappointed because I thought I'd at least be able to hear the water. But it sounded like she was in a bar or something. Just lots of people laughing and glasses clinking and stupid music.

"So, how's the research?" I ask her.

"Sorry, honey, I can't hear you that well" is what she says. Oh, well. At least she calls.

When I moan about this, Old Henry just says, *"Your happiness is entwined with your outlook on life."* Hmmph! He must have been born in a fortune-cookie factory. He can be kind of exasperating sometimes. When I ask him what he means by that, he merely says, *"More pineapple, please!"* and smiles like a mysterious Buddha.

As I stare out the windows here on top of the world in my own private cupola (well . . . nobody ELSE comes up here, except Oliver), I see someone way out on what Grandpa calls "the flats." That's when the tide goes out and leaves this really long stretch of smelly mud. The person is all hunched over. It's someone in overalls and shockingly large boots. I think the person is a girl. She is doing something with a stick and a plastic sled. I think she might even be Mad, whose name is probably Madeleine. If I had a name that cool, I'd use it.

"Oliver," I say—because (besides Old Henry) it's who I mainly converse with these days—"not that you aren't terribly entertaining, but I need to find out who that is."

Let's face it. I'm only thirteen, and I can't spend my days talking only to a cat and the outside of my brother's door.

This is how I meet Madeleine. First, I waltz outside into yellow air. Yellow air is normal around here. The morning fog burns off, and still it isn't quite clear. The air holds the sunlight like water takes on color. I like it. I'm walking in gold.

The person is still out in the mud, busily bending and scratching around. I just stand at the top of the cliff watching her. Then she turns and walks toward shore, hauling that funny pink sled behind her. From here I hear the mudflats pulling at her boots like they want to keep her. *Schluup. Schluup. Schluup.* Grandpa says there are honeypots out there, holes that will suck you right down. But the girl keeps on walking with her sled. I make my way down the cliff path to the shore. It's hard wearing flip-flops.

The person looks up and sees me and waves a little princess wave. Not that she's any kind of elegant in those waist-high boots and overalls. Plus, she's covered in mud. I wave back.

Thorne claims he likes it.
I say it's cat
torture.

Oliver listens to technopop.
(Thorne says it's techno-ROCK.)
(So I say POP, just to bug him.)

Then I stand around waiting because there's no way I'm going out into the mud. It's not just the honeypots, it's my flip-flops. They are all wrong. (Who would wear flip-flops out onto the mudflats?) In this case the right shoes seem to be green boots that go up to your chest. Your very large chest, in the case of this person: tall, big, and blond.

The pink sled bumps behind her, all mucky with what must be uncleaned clams. I want to know all about clamming, but without asking. Being new everywhere all the time is a pain. There's always tons of stuff I don't know. I hate being clueless, but half the time I am. I ask the stupidest questions. Like all those orange caps at the Quikstop? I asked Helen why orange was so in up here, and she and Delwyn just about fell over. Hunting is the reason, didn't I know? "You wear orange so you don't get mistaken for a deer and shot."

Duh.

Thorne usually knows stuff, which annoys me, but it *is* kind of useful, like living with an interpreter. But I don't think he's come outside more than three times since we've been here! Useless. . . .

"Hello," I call to the girl I think is Mad but I'm not sure. Why can't I just know things by OSMOSIS? We studied that in science this spring. *Osmosis:* the passage of particles through a membrane from areas of high concentration to low . . . the passage of words into my brain from the world to ME!

She keeps walking toward me, the sled bucking over the big rocks on the beach.

"Hi," says the girl, wiping her forehead and leaving a long muddy streak.

"Hi," I reply, folding my arms in front of my scrawny self (due to the nippy wind and all).

"You must be Aggie," she says, matter-of-factly.

I nod. She knows. Well, why shouldn't she? She must shop at the Quikstop. I begin to sense that there's probably a terrible lack of privacy around here. But so what? I acknowledge my dreadful name. I resist the temptation to tell her it is really pronounced "Agathe" with sort of a French accent.

"I'm Mad."

I just knew it.

We stand there by the mudflats. I'm scrolling through my brain, thinking of what to say next, when the silence is interrupted.

A huge white cat with brown and orange spots comes yowling down the beach.

"Do you like cats?" asks Mad, draping this one around her neck. A live yowling scarf.

"I haven't known that many," I say. "Only Grandpa's cat, Oliver. I like Oliver."

"Here," says Mad. "Let Penelope visit you." And she lifts Penelope off her shoulder and onto mine. But Penelope is not pleased. She squirms around to the back of my awfully bare neck and hangs there, clawing for dear life. It stings like a river of bees. I fling off Penelope, clutching at my neck. Mad looks shocked. She wants to know if I'm okay, if I want that burning lotion that moms insist on for scraped knees. But I don't want that. The only thing I want is her for a friend, so I say, "Naaah. I'm fine." I could win the Academy Award for that line, because really my neck is killing me.

"I'm sooo sorry," says Mad as Penelope stalks off.

My powers of prediction say this: Penelope the cat and I are enemies for life. I bet Penelope hunts and kills birds, for example, and I love birds.

But Mad and I will be friends, although she's probably fifteen. I nod good-bye, kind of cool-like, as Mad walks toward the house at the end of the beach. I thought that must be her house. I saw a tall, blond woman hanging laundry there the other day, like a grown-up version of Mad.

Mad and Penelope

Mad doesn't ask me to follow her. I begin to wish I'd said I needed that lotion. I wish I'd asked Mad about clamming. Maybe I could go with her sometime soon and vary our fish-fish-and-more-fish diet a little.

But I just go up the hill to Grandpa's to wash my neck.

When Mom calls, I tell her.

"I think I met a friend today."

"Yes?" says my mother, but sounding kind of distracted. My radar switches on.

"Who's that in the background?" I demand.

"Oh, nobody." She pauses. "Well, actually, his name is Ian." She giggles, and there's a muffled sound.

I hate it when she acts like one of her dopey characters.

"Tell me about your new friend," she says, practicing the mom-like behavior that so often eludes her.

"NEVER MIND," I say, just to bug her.

"How did you meet?" She persists, the annoying murmuring still coming through loud and clear. Maybe Ian is nibbling her earlobes. Blech!

"Her cat gave me lifelong scars and probably cat scratch fever," I say, even though I have no idea what cat scratch fever is. Then for some reason I start laughing hysterically and hang up.

I wait for her to call back, but she doesn't.

Up in the cupola (did I mention it was good for moping?) I pull Old Henry out of my pocket. My neck feels terrible, despite the lotion Grandpa insisted on when I showed him what happened. Oliver's up here too, putting in a good word for cat behavior of the nonpsychotic kind.

"*A friend is golden,*" says Old Henry.

"I don't have any friends," I say to him, and realize for a moment that this might be true. It's been months

Grandpa's House —
it's huge, but has
seen better days!

since I got a letter from Isla (I'm pretty hard to keep track of, so I can't blame her). Leslie Mender, my only real friend from Port Chester, wants me to e-mail her, but Grandpa doesn't even have a microwave, let alone a computer!

I look out to sea, feeling sorry for myself. A boat is thunking past, followed by a cloud of hungry gulls. The sky is pink. All this beauty somehow makes the feeling worse.

"Destiny is chosen," Old Henry throws in for good measure.

He can be worse than any mom.

When I finally go down to see if I can at least torment Thorne (to make myself feel better), Grandpa is doing it for me.

"So, just how much sleep do you need, young man?" Grandpa is asking Thorne. An innocent question but with a lot of baggage. In other words, "Are you a lazy bum, or is it just my imagination?"

Thorne doesn't look so good. He's slouched on the end of the nubby floral armchair, otherwise known as Oliver's scratching post. Grandpa's standing. Thorne has one pant leg stuffed into his sock. Frankly, it looks demented. Thorne usually cares about his look, goofy as it is. This is not a good sign.

"Teenagers need a lot of sleep, Grandpa," I say, seeing as how Thorne isn't saying a word. In fact, I don't remember hearing him speak for the last three days. I give his leg a little nudge. Oliver, the ever-kind (polar opposite of Penelope), jumps up onto Thorne's lap and starts purring his motorboat purr. We're coming to his rescue, and to watch Grandpa go after Thorne, but he doesn't. Instead Grandpa collapses in slow motion to the floor. He bends over funny, and I wonder if this is some kind of symptom of a stroke. Thorne and I look at each other, shocked.

Grandpa removes his left shoe. He has an odd expression on his face. Then he bends his long, creaky left leg up to his ear, which I'm not even sure I could do, and I'm pretty limber.

Then, with a strange look on his face, he starts talking.

"Hello?" says Grandpa, into his own foot.

"Oh, it's you."

"Yes, they're fine."

That's Grandpa talking . . . with long pauses in between. Thorne and I are just too stunned to do anything but listen. I take the opportunity to fix Thorne's tucked-in pant leg, and he doesn't even react.

"Well that's just fine, de-ah," says Grandpa, chuckling at something. "I'll tell them."

He puts down his leg like he's hanging up a phone. He gives his shin a quick little massage. Then, as calmly as if he took phone calls on his leg every day, Grandpa puts on his shoe.

"That was Meredith," he says, "your mom. . . ." (Like we'd forget!)

"She's not coming back for a while."

Thorne and I look at each other. It's hard to know what to make of a message delivered care of your grandfather's leg. That old tree crow might as well have swooped in with a message from Mom in its beak. That would just seem more likely.

But on cue both Thorne and I say, "Okay."

It's the kind of message we were probably expecting anyhow.

stuck in my throat, but it's just that lump that comes sometimes when I'm trying not to cry.

I turn to look at Grandpa, but he's asleep in the rocker, his telephonic leg just nudging the floor.

"Friggin' Mom," says Thorne, as if he's lived here all his life.

June 20

The weird thing is, Mom calls us the very next day. Right in the middle of supper, as usual. That's her knack. We could eat at any hour and she'd call right then. We're having Grandpa's chowder, which is a lovely dish, if you don't mind practically drinking butter. I don't. (Thorne does.)

She talks to Thorne first. He listens, raises an eyebrow at me, then says to her, "I know."

He hands me the phone.

We chitchat for a minute about how she and Ian went miniature golfing and about how my new favorite drink is Moxie. Then she says, "I've decided I need to remain on site for a few more weeks. Think you can handle staying with Grandpa?"

Yipes.

I look at Thorne.

He rolls his eyes and shrugs.

"Um, sure," I tell her, after a lot of dead air. She can have Niagara and Ian too.

"We'll be fine," I tell her. Mom wants to talk to Thorne again, but he gives me the "no way" sign, so I lie and say he's left the table. I hang up, and it feels like I have foc

June 22

As it turns out, Grandpa starts getting phone calls fast and furious. They aren't always from Mom. One is from the Queen Mum in England, who I feel pretty sure is dead. One's from William Carlos Williams, who wrote that poem about how so much depends upon a red wheelbarrow glazed with rain water beside the white chickens. And he is DEFINITELY dead. Still, Grandpa should ask him about that wheelbarrow. If it's so important, what's it doing out there in the rain?

Sometimes it gets even weirder. Grandpa thinks the phone in his leg is also some kind of listening device and that he, Eugene Bellicose, is being wiretapped.

"Oh, yes," says Grandpa. "I've been this way ever since my accident. I had to have my knee fixed up on account of the tractor falling on it. I guess I must have been lying in that field for hours until Delwyn happened by. That ornery crow invited all his cackling friends, and they told me the worst jokes."

We nod, which is what you are supposed to do with crazy people. Don't argue. But when Grandpa starts telling us about the surveillance part, we just have to ask some questions.

"Like in a James Bond movie?" asks Thorne.

"Exactly," says Grandpa, all serious.

"Paranoia," mutters Thorne under his breath.

"The Icelandic Army," whispers Grandpa, as if he shouldn't be detected saying that. "They are coming."

"But Iceland is a small, peaceful island nation," says Thorne, rising to the occasion.

"With no trees," I add, although I don't know what that has to do with anything. But whatever we say doesn't make a difference to Grandpa. He hears what he hears. He thinks what he thinks. And he keeps getting calls from the Icelandic Army, which is preparing to invade. To invade Small Cove, of all places! Even Ludwig is just barely on the map.

"How come you understand Icelandic?" I ask him. But I stay polite about it.

From up here in the cupola,
I have a superior perspective!

June 24

We've been here for three weeks, which is a very short
time and a very long time. I'm used to the bell buoy now
and all the quiet. Thanks to Delwyn and "the boys," I
have figured out the rules of cribbage. Thanks to Helen,
I know a few things about my grandmother, the one I
resemble. It turns out her name was AGATHA! That's the
sort of thing I think Mom could have told me herself.
JEEZ LOUISE, like Delwyn would say. Anyhow, I'm
going to find out more about the other Agatha.

I have stopped trying to figure out Grandpa. He's so
eccentric it's practically predictable. He sleeps off and on
through the day but not much at night. Sometimes when
I get up to pee, he is out chopping wood in the dark.
Sometimes he is sitting at the kitchen table doing his
puzzles. They are always mysteriously gone in the morning. You'd think he'd make more headway if he just left
the puzzle out and kept working on it. Last night I
couldn't sleep, so he and I worked on a lighthouse puzzle.
I figured out a lot of the sky. While we were working,
Grandpa asked me if I'd like to keep chickens.

"But, Grandpa," I say, "the chicken coop is falling
down."

"Ayuh. Haven't been any chickens there since your mother left and the Big Storm blew the whole gang clear across to Toothaker's Point."

"You're kidding!"

"Nope. Never do."

I close my eyes for a second, imagining chickens whirling through a storm, blown like leaves straight over the water. Like Dorothy to Oz.

"You never got 'em back?" I ask.

"Nah. Before long, just about all of them were eaten by the fox, or by Old Toothaker himself. Couldn't get myself to care, with your mother gone off and all the rest of it."

"What rest of it?" I say.

But Grandpa just picks at the puzzle pieces. It's two o'clock in the morning. I should probably go back to bed.

"Toothaker's daughter still keeps a few. You know her? Minnie Toothaker? Big as a house."

I shake my head. How would I know anyone unless they ate at the Quikstop? Grandpa's eyes get that lost look. We work on in silence until I just have to go to bed.

"With enough wind, chickens can fly," says Old Henry when I take him out to give him a good-night kiss. *"Even over water."*

June 25

This morning, the puzzle is gone again, and Grandpa doesn't say anything else about chickens. I go out and stand by the chicken coop. It looks like it's about to slide down the cliff. I pick up some of the chicken wire that has fallen off its post and hitch it back up. I pound a loose nail back in with a rock. Because with Grandpa, you just never know.

Cribbage and puzzles and chicken coops are good, but the best thing is, Mad is done with school and she actually seems to want to hang out with me! She showed up at the kitchen door this morning, wearing a T-shirt that said FURBISH LOUSEWORT. It turns out that Furbish Lousewort is NOT the name of a rock band like what I first thought. It's this scrawny plant, and Emma Furbish discovered it for the first time someplace not too far from here. So the plant got her name and it's important, even though it's not in the least bit gorgeous, judging from the faded picture on Mad's shirt. I feel a bit funny, staring at her chest. Mad's definitely got boobs, unlike me. If I have anything, I have tits. That's how I think of it. The letters in BOOB are round and big. The letters in tit are skinny. Like me. Anyhow, a tit is a kind of bird, and, as I've said, I like birds. (So does Grandpa!)

Mad likes plants. A lot! And not just on T-shirts. It turns out she's some kind of naturalist. When she came to the kitchen door, she wanted me to go fiddleheading with her. I said sure, I'd go, but I had absolutely 100 percent NO IDEA what she was talking about. I hoped it didn't have to do with actual fiddles, because (unlike Thorne) I'm a-musical. I can't even hum right.

But it turns out that fiddleheads are a kind of fern. Ferns you can eat. You cut them on little islands in the middle of rivers and streams like the one that rushes out back behind Our Lady of the Wilderness Church. The running water's even colder than the ocean.

"All snow melt," explains Mad, although it's already June.

I had to borrow Mad's brother's boots so I could go fiddleheading. He's away at college, I guess. His name is Steve. Thorne didn't want to come, although Mad asked him. She walked right up to him as he was smoking by the rosebushes. He actually took off his headphones and talked to her, but he didn't want to go. I'm just as glad. I don't really feel like sharing her, quite frankly.

"Thorne's wicked cute," Mad tells me as she shows me fiddleheads and how they grow all curled up.

She may have unbelievably bad taste, but she's still my friend.

Speaking of bad taste, I pop one of the fiddleheads in my mouth. This thing's bitter and stringy, and I spit it right out. Mad practically falls into the stream laughing.

"You're supposed to boil them!" She laughs. "And eat 'em with butter and salt. Not *raw*, you kook."

I don't mind if she calls me a kook. I just smile.

We pick so many fiddleheads that the colander Mad brought doesn't do it. We put the rest of the crop in Mad's Red Sox cap and bring it up to Grandpa. He beams at us. And that night Mad and I make dinner: noodles with garlic and cooked fiddleheads.

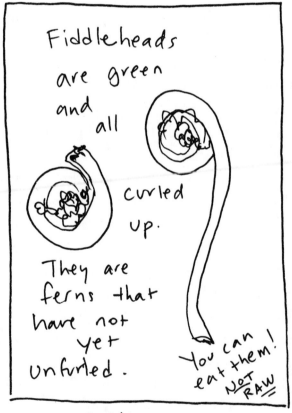

Fiddleheads

"Somewhat like asparagus," says Thorne, who likes to describe food.

"Yup," I say, "but with the hint of a bitter aftertaste." He nods. Sometimes he doesn't know I'm teasing him, and that makes me love him even more. But I won't tell him that. I just wish he'd start liking it up here. Even with Mad sitting right next to him, paying him all kinds of attention, he's chewing his thumb. That's what he does when he's miserable.

"Tell me about Grandma," I say to Grandpa. Tonight's puzzle is impossible.

But Grandpa doesn't say a word, only sighs.

"Tell me about chickens, then," I say.

Grandpa concentrates on the background forest for a few minutes. There are about four hundred pieces that are various shades of green and almost all the same shape.

"Chickens don't lay if they ain't happy," he says, finally. But he doesn't mention anything about getting any.

Strangely enough, I'm kind of disappointed. I decide to start patching up the coop for real. It just looks too empty and sad.

June 26

Mad says she'll take me swimming. Yes! Now we're talking. It's not that I don't want to spend all my time tromp-
ing through bushes looking for specimens and being
eaten alive by mosquitoes, it's just that I prefer swimming! She says she saw me that first day I swam. I blush,
remembering my spastic dive.

"Nobody goes swimming in Small Cove," she says matter-of-factly. "I'll show you a much better place." She
explains that Small Cove is fairly open water and that's
why it stays so cold. "Anywhere we go is going to be cold
this early," she says. "But at least it will be better."

I'm embarrassed to be wearing my old pink bathing
suit. Next time Mom calls I'm going to insist on a new
suit, not to mention hiking boots.

As we walk, Mad points out plants. There are these
really awesome ones called lady's slippers. "A native
orchid," explains my local botanist. These are pink and
white flowers, so beautiful I almost can't believe it. They
really do look like dangling ballet slippers.

"Or a scrotum," says Mad, who seems to use a lot of
scientific words.

We walk for about fifteen minutes down the rocky

coast from Small Cove. We walk past the funny little trailer that sits on the edge of Grandpa's property and stick our heads in. It smells like cat pee.

"Your grandma used to live here when I was a kid," says Mad, as we back out. "She moved out on your

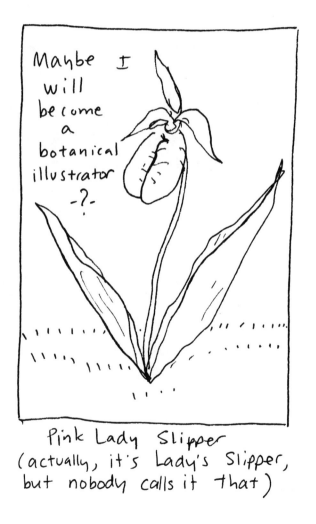

Maybe I will become a botanical illustrator -?-

Pink Lady Slipper
(actually, it's Lady's Slipper,
but nobody calls it that)

grandpa when he started trying to get rid of bats with his shotgun. I used to be kind of afraid of your grandpa, actually. But he seems a lot more mellow now. His wife was nice. She kept the most amazing African violets right here in the trailer. She'd give me molasses cookies just about every time I came to see her. But then she moved away."

"Actually," I tell Mad, "that must have been Eileen you met. Grandpa's second wife. My *real* grandma, Agatha, has been dead for a long time." And even though it's very sad, I feel happy talking about Grandma Agatha, saying her name.

We follow the rocky path. I've left my flip-flops on a rock and am practicing toughening up my feet. There's something in the air that makes me glad, makes me almost giddy (which is like being glad but on high speed). I tell Mad and she says, "Negative ions. Air by the ocean is rich in it."

I nod as if I know all about how something negative could be so positive.

We turn the corner and climb down a hill, grasping at roots to keep us from sliding.

"Welcome to Nowhere Cove," says Mad, flinging her arms open wide.

We swim, and it IS much warmer. Afterward, Mad and I sit on the hillside, thawing out. I'm a much better swimmer than she is, and she noticed. But that's not what we talk about. We're looking out to sea. There's an island out there, not too far away. It's just a bump of an island with a small stand of trees. But there seems to be a house or something on it. I noticed the island from the cupola but never saw the house. I ask Mad.

"Oh, that's Cat Island," she says, and she looks at me kind of funny, as if I should know. Mad pulls her sweatshirt over her knees. The wind is brisk. The moon has risen up above the rim of sea, although it's still afternoon. "It's really called Halfway Rock, but there was a mean old lady who used to take every litter her cat had and tie 'em up out there. Rita Scarp was her name. What a witch. She rowed herself out. Nobody could ever catch her at it, but everybody knew. She's been dead for years. You can still find kitten bones among the rocks. It's kind of spooky. The house is just left over from a long time ago. Your grandpa might know who built it. I don't remember."

"I could practically swim to Cat Island from here," I say, bragging. She just laughs at me. It's a great feeling, sucking up the heat of the warm bare rock, talking with my friend Mad.

When my mom calls, I tell her about swimming with Mad in Nowhere Cove.

"I know which cove that is," says Mom. "The trailer cove. I used to call it Lost Cove, because I thought only my friends and I went there." It turns out she knows all about Cat Island and Rita Scarp and everything. "Such a

sad place," she says, and goes quiet. But I feel happy and generous, and so I ask her about Ian. I don't usually like to encourage the boyfriend business.

"Oh . . . him," she says in a not-so-pumped-up voice. "Forget about him, honey. He was nobody."

"So are you coming back soon?" I ask, to fill the silence and because I want to know.

"Soon," she promises.

Sometimes I feel a little sorry for my mom.

But at least right now I don't feel sorry for me.

Maybe being a grown-up isn't that easy....

June 27

I may be doing okay, but Thorne remains a thorny issue. He hates it when I say that, so I do it all the time. He chews his thumb until it's raw. He stays in his room. He hasn't cooked his famous pasta sauce once, even though I put a box of linguini right on the table.

Even Grandpa's on to him. When we were working on last night's puzzle (an Impressionist bouquet), he said to me, "So, this brother of yours . . ." Then his voice just trailed off and we worked on the impossible blue vase. But I knew something was going to happen.

Something happens.

This morning about eleven there's a rapping on the door while we are all drinking tea. I'm glad Thorne is up, wearing his tea cozy hat and slurping away with us. I've become a big tea drinker. I ask Thorne if we could maybe borrow his hat to keep the pot warm, and this makes Grandpa laugh and Thorne scowl, as usual.

"Enter," calls Grandpa as Delwyn walks in, huffing and puffing from riding his bicycle up our hill. I'm not used to seeing him anyplace but the Quikstop, so he looks kind of funny in Grandpa's kitchen.

"Tea, Delwyn?" asks Grandpa.

"Don't mind if I do, de-ah," Delwyn says. (That's a funny part about being up here: Grown men call each other—and everybody else!—dear.)

"How's Helen?" asks Grandpa.

"Oh, Mothah's fine," Delwyn says, and nods. "Just fine."

So Delwyn joins us at the table. Pretty soon it's marmalade toast all around, although we have to make it on the woodstove, since Grandpa doesn't have a toaster. Grandpa calls the woodstove a "cookstove" and doesn't bother much with the electric one.

"So," says Delwyn, dabbing at his upper lip with his handkerchief. "I'm here to talk with Thorne."

Thorne looks very surprised but doesn't say a thing.

It turns out that Delwyn is looking for someone to help out with the church.

"We're in between pastors," explains Delwyn. "But I've got the key up at the Quikstop. I'm keeping an eye on the place until they send us someone . . . maybe later in the summer is what I heard."

And it turns out he needs help with mowing and such now that it's summer. Someone to sweep up the cobwebs.

"I'm not so spry anymore, you know," Delwyn says, and winks at us.

We sit there for a while, drinking tea.

"I think I could do that," says Thorne, as if he'd been a handyman all his life. I can't remember him ever having any kind of job, except paperboy for a few months when we lived in New Jersey.

"Wonders never cease," mumbles Grandpa, gazing at the ceiling.

"Good," says Delwyn. "The key's behind the counter. We had to start locking it last summer when those kids from town came out and spray-painted their nonsense all around the place."

And that's that, apparently. I sit there refraining from mentioning that besides the time we went to mom's friend Brie's wedding, I don't think Thorne's EVER set foot in a church. Me neither. But I guess there's a difference between sweeping and believing, anyhow.

So Thorne is transformed over tea and toast from guy-who-stays-locked-in-his-room to what Grandpa calls the church sexton. He's going to get paid too.

"It'll be good for you," Grandpa insists, and Thorne sucks in some Maine air and says, "Ayuh."

June 28

Thorne starts the next day. I can already see a plus to this job: It gets him out of bed. I walk up with him to the Quikstop, but then Delwyn takes the key down from its little hook and they go over, and I think I should probably leave them alone. What am I, his mother? Besides, I can see him through the window from the lunch counter.

So I stay, drinking my first Moxie of the day. It's interesting listening to people talk. Two ancient lobstermen with faces like wrinkled roadmaps are eating ham and eggs and talking about how some guy traded his wife for a hunting dog. They are Orren and Harlen Coffin, old bachelor brothers who take a lot of their meals right here at the Quikstop. They both wear bright orange suspenders. They're part of the cribbage club. Through the window I see Delwyn and Thorne walking around Our Lady. Delwyn's gesturing at bushes and windows. Thorne's nodding and writing stuff in his little notebook. He's like Mom and me that way. He always has a notebook. Most of his stuff is supposedly song lyrics. I look at them sometimes. They're not songs I would sing, but everyone's different.

* * *

*I can't seem to draw Cat Island.
It should look far and close
at the same time.*

Mad's not around, so I decide to go up to my cupola. I haven't had enough time to draw lately, with all the swimming, botanizing, and chicken coop repair I seem to do around here. I got Grandpa to give me a hammer and nails, and I'm slapping the boards back up. (So far no word on chickens, and I guess that's okay, since their house is a mess.) I look down at my notebook and back out to sea. I'm concentrating on Cat Island to see if I can get a sense of distance into my picture.

"*The world is your oyster,*" says Old Henry, who is dancing around on the page as he often does.

"The world is my sardine," I agree, chewing on the pencil, admiring the long, blue view.

But I'm too distracted. For some reason Cat Island is giving me the creeps. I stop trying to draw it and decide to go find Mad. Maybe she'll come with me up to Our Lady of the Wilderness to see Thorne.

But the real lady of the wilderness appears to be Mad. She's not around.

"She put on her hiking boots this morning," says Mad's mother, who always tells me to call her Solveig. She's Norwegian and looks it (if you think tall, blond, and gorgeous). "And she packed a lunch."

By now I know that means she'll be gone awhile. I would be annoyed that Mad didn't ask me, but it's just too weird to be jealous of wildflowers. Solveig talks with clothespins in her teeth. She's hanging the laundry. Her underwear, or maybe Mad's, flits nonchalantly in the breeze. A whole lot of bras. I don't have a single one! No matter where I end up going to school this fall, Mom better take me shopping. Bras are one of the few things they don't actually sell up at the Quikstop, and even if they did, there's no way I'd buy one right in public.

Grandpa says that Mad's family are such bright

people, they'll hang their laundry in the rain. He says this in a superior sort of voice. And they do. Hang it when it's sprinkling, that is. I've seen them.

"Well," I say to Grandpa, "at least they DO laundry." Ours is lying around in piles. I've taken to washing my undies in the upstairs sink.

Grandpa closes his eyes and begins to snore almost immediately. I decide to go up to the church.

The natives are strange, but I like them!

* * *

I see Thorne in the little graveyard. It looks like he's taking a break from mowing. He's sitting on a gravestone (are you supposed to do that?), smoking, and writing in his notebook.

"Hey, Aggie," he says without looking up.

"Hey, Thorne," I answer, and walk back to the stream where Grandma's headstone is. Agatha Jane Bellicose, 1937–1978. I come here a lot since Helen showed me the stone. It's smooth and gray. Thorne says granite. I run my hand over the cool top and wonder about Grandma.

I wander back to Thorne. He's still writing away.

It's a totally hot day, at least for the moment. What Delwyn says about the weather is true: If you don't like it, wait a couple of minutes. Fog, sun, wind, rain. We could probably even get snow! I'm all sweaty from my dash up the dirt road. You have to run through a salt marsh, and I mean run. Salt marsh mosquitoes make the regular kind look like wimps.

"Whatcha doing?" I ask, wanting to stub out the cigarette. What if he set the place on fire? Plus, it stinks. Also, it kills you.

"Emphysema," I say, but he still doesn't look up.

I sit down next to him and realize we're in a wild strawberry patch. Mad showed me how you can pick the little berries and thread them on a straw of grass. It's a Scandinavian thing.

I sit there threading. Thorne keeps writing. I might as well be on the moon. But that's okay. *Scritch, scritch, scratch* goes his pen. He just writes. I'm the only one who draws. I lean over, pretending it's to offer him some strawberries.

"Hey," he says, and closes the book.

"Strawberry?" I ask.

"Sure," he says, putting out his cigarette and pocketing the stub. At least he isn't a litterbug. Then he gobbles down my entire offering, sixteen tiny strawberries and the grass straw too!

"Thorne," I yell, punching him. "That's not how the Norwegians do it! You're supposed to eat ONE berry at a time. Idiot."

He looks at me, smiling. "I needed a chlorophyll fix . . . and fiber. It's all the fish we've been eating."

I punch him again. He punches me. We're rolling around laughing, about to crack our skulls open on these old stones, when a beat-up truck slows down. We stop wrestling. Is it acceptable to wrestle in cemeteries?

A guy leans out the window and calls, "Hey, Thorne, who's the chick?"

I sit back on my heels, pushing my overly long bangs out of my face, blushing my head off. Of course. I suffer from CBS: Constant Blushing Syndrome. Because this someone is a guy, maybe Thorne's age but not so dorky looking, and guys make me feel kind of edgy and shy. I narrow my eyes.

"Hey," says Thorne as if he has a social life and actually knows this person.

The guy gets out of the truck. For some reason he leaves it running like someone who wants to be able to make a quick getaway.

"You must be Aggie," he says.

"Of course I am," I reply, hands on my hips.

"Tucker Toothaker," he says, looking back and forth from Thorne to me. "And you two look some alike. Except sister here is cuter." I blush again and look at my feet. Maybe he'll think I have some sort of sunburn. And did he just say his name was Toothaker? That's almost as bad as Aggie. I wonder if he's related to my chickens? Wasn't Grandpa going to get them from Toothaker's? I stare at his feet for a while. He's wearing work boots, the kind with steel toes. You can tell a lot about people just by looking at their feet. I'm still in the stupid flip-flops. I will myself to look up. I make it to his T-shirt, which reads EXPECT A MACKEREL.

And he must see me squinching my eyes, not quite getting it, because he says, "You know, like 'expect a miracle,' only different." We all laugh. "And speaking of miracles, you gonna give us a tour?" He nods over toward the church.

"What? You haven't been in it?" Thorne asks, pretending to be shocked.

"Well, yah, my sister got married, but that was before that graffiti thing, and didn't Helen's niece the artist come and decorate it up some? Haley?"

"Yes," says Thorne, local history expert. "It's actually really cool."

Haley Wing - the Artist
(I hope we're related somehow)

"Well, let's see it," says Tucker, and we all walk in. I'm thinking nobody told me Haley was Helen's niece, but I guess that's just the way it is up here.

This place is unbelievable! Why didn't Thorne drag me down here the minute he first saw it? I give him a little kick. He doesn't even flinch, he's so used to that sort of stuff, but I believe he knows exactly what I mean. I didn't know churches could be like this! The ones in the movies always have rows of seats, a few stained-glass windows, and the altar up on a stage. But *this* is really different. There are all kinds of statues in here sticking out from little alcoves, balancing on tables, populating the place. But it's not Jesus or the wise men or any of the usual stuff. These are big carvings of animals and flowers. I feel like I'm in a fairy-tale forest. No wonder it's called Our Lady of the WILDERNESS! Everything is painted gold and blue and red. There are even animals up on the wall, carved animal heads that stick out really high above us, sort of like stuffed moose heads, only not at all like that. There is one woman in a long blue robe, gazing upward toward some little yellow birds. This is probably the Virgin Mary, but to me it looks like Mad. Maybe that's who Haley used as a model.

I stand in a beam of sunlight, practically holding my breath. Here I do expect a miracle. It's so beautiful. Who would have guessed that all this could be found inside such a tidy box of a building? It's like finding out your strictest teacher likes punk rock.

"Wow," says Tucker, finally. "Cool."

"So, do people come?" I ask them. "I mean, is this a museum or really a church?"

"How should I know?" asks Thorne. "I only sweep here."

"Helen says the Reverend Evelyn is scheduled for sometime next month. She comes on a motorcycle," Tucker says. "That's what I heard."

"Yeah?" asks Thorne.

"Harley," says Tucker, reverently.

And that reminds me, "You left your truck running, you know." I give myself BIG points for talking to him. I bet he's probably seventeen.

"Oh yeah." He grins at me. "So let's go."

"Sure," says Thorne. "Just wait while I lock up." And we walk around, all official-like. If Thorne's going, I'm going too. I walk out to the truck and jump in as if I'm the kind of girl who does that sort of thing. Rides around with guys in trucks. This one has a bumper sticker that says QUIT YUR BEEFING—EAT LOBSTER. The truck, that is, not the guy.

I'm wedged between Tucker and Thorne. I can't help it if my leg is smushed up next to Tucker's. I don't know how he's going to shift without bashing into me. I sit there making myself small and acting casual. I wonder what Mad thinks of Tucker. I start wishing she were here too. At least Thorne is. And there's a big wet nose in my ear.

I turn around. Through the open window of the cab, a sweet old retriever is nosing me.

"That's Goldy," says Tucker. "Lie down, girl." We pull out with a screech. I look back at Goldy, who's lying down, unphased. She's probably used to careening around. As we race off, I notice the lawn mower, abandoned among the long weeds, the cemetery half-mown and waiting.

"Now for some more religious art," says Tucker. "People down here are real serious about their lawn doodads."

And I know what he means. There's stuff on everyone's lawn, just about.

"In fact," says Tucker—his big dog breathes in my ear—
"Sit down, Goldy. In fact, this is the lawn ornament capital
of North America." And he proceeds to give us a tour.

"On your right, ladies and gentlemen, you will see an
exquisite example of an early garden gnome. Its owners,
the lovely Heidi and Harry Rideout, take good care of
their art, yessir. Every winter, they bring the little fellow

right up into their den and dress him in Christmas lights. I happen to know, since Heidi is my very own sister."

We wave at the gnome. "Hi, Bob!" Thorne calls out the window, and we all laugh.

"Just across the street here, in front of this maaagnificent log cabin, which in case you're interested has been under construction since before I was born, there is a most delightful seagull. Take a look at those rotating wings." And he goes on and on like that. We drive up and down and all around leafy green and carsick roads, seeing stuff. Pink flamingoes. Cutouts of wooden ladies with really big butts, bending over in gardens. "Notice that some have polka-dot skirts and others wear plain. . . . The two kinds don't talk to each other," says Tucker, grinning sideways at me. (I blush yet again.)

"And very popular this year are the metallic gazing balls. So what else is new?" continues Tucker Toothaker, local art critic. He's pointing at stuff right and left. Sometimes he has *neither* hand on the steering wheel.

We count three gazing balls in silver, two in green, and several pinks.

"Of course, some people just go in for flags," says Thorne.

"Ayuh," grins Tucker, taking another corner way too fast. I swear he's doing it just so he can fall over on me. I brace myself so I don't touch him when we turn left. It's like a silent battle we're having, but I kind of don't mind losing. We drive by a gathering of off-duty Christmas ornaments: two Santas, several reindeer, and one snow-man, with an Easter bunny thrown in for good measure.

Tucker glances at us. "It's always friggin' Christmas at the Joneses'," he says.

We drive by a barn that looks like it has been falling down for years. We drive by trees and more trees. We're way out of Ludwig now. Even I can tell that. Tucker pulls up in front of a small white cape.

"And now for the grand finale," he says. "What you see before you might look like an ordinary Mary." It's a blue-robed statue, maybe three feet high, standing in an upended bathtub, surrounded by violets. She's kind of pretty, with her palm, white as snow, outstretched to meet us.

"Those people must be Catholic," I say. Duh. So obvious.

"And not only that," adds Tucker. "They are good care-takers of religious art. Like Thorne here." And he laughs a sarcastic laugh. Suddenly, I get this sick feeling that Tucker had something to do with spray-painting the church. I don't know why. Sometimes the pit of my stom-ach just talks to me. I lean way over on Thorne, wonder-ing why I came.

"Every winter the Whynots here wrap her up good in plastic garbage bags and tie her up with rope to protect her from the mighty elements. I've seen it since I was a kid riding the bus to school."

"The virgin in bondage?" laughs Thorne.

"Exactly," says Tucker. "You can tell it's summer by the fact that she's unwrapped. Only happened about three weeks ago. You can never trust spring around here." He revs the engine, and we tear off past the trees and the rows and rows of mailboxes.

On the way home, Tucker slows the truck by the house with the four pink flamingoes and tells Thorne to grab one.

"Go ahead, just scoop it up. It won't bite."

"What?" asks Thorne, kind of flustered.

"Don't worry about it. That's my uncle's house. I play tricks on him all the time."

Thorne leans out the window and grabs the bird by the neck. He tosses it back with the sleeping Goldy as if he'd been pinching lawn art all his life.

"We're just going to shake things up a little," explains Tucker. At the next house, he tells Thorne to put the flamingo on the lawn but take the silver gazing ball off its pedestal. He has to get out to do it. It's broad daylight. I slump down in the seat. I'm not sure I like this game.

But Tucker and Thorne are having the time of their lives. We switch chipmunks for plastic skunks, dog cutouts for big-butt ladies. We take a leftover Easter bunny and replace it with a little Dutch boy. It's a good thing it's so hot that nobody's out in their front yards.

"Ah, they're all watching TV," says Tucker when I worry out loud. He drops us off in front of the church. Thorne's got to go back to mowing, it seems. I wave good-bye as I trot back down toward the mosquito marsh. I was thinking I'd get a Moxie, but I have too much guilt on my face. Guilt and pimples . . . such an award-winning combination. Helen would know for sure that I was involved in the Great Lawn Ornament Mix-up! People must be calling her by now.

Thorne and Tucker wave back at me. I wonder what they'll do next. I'm not sure I want to know, except Thorne had BETTER tell me.

Anyway, I like Goldy the dog.

Lawn Doodads :

Help! I'm just an innocent gnome

Big-Butt Ladies do not have heads.

Gazing balls come in many colors. If you own one, you are being controlled by aliens (says Thorne). (I believe him.)

Wings flap in breeze

I would call them DON'T dads !

July

July 1

Mom doesn't call again tonight. That makes seven days. One whole week. Thorne tries the number for the motel where she is supposedly staying, but they say she's checked out.

"Maybe she's on her way back," I say, but I don't really believe it.

"Maybe." Thorne shrugs. Then he criticizes me for not rinsing the pots off enough. "You expect me to put these greasy things back in the cupboard?"

I look at Grandpa. Grandpa's napping by the cookstove with Oliver in his lap. Somehow I don't want to get mad at Thorne, even if he thinks he's Mr. Cool Employed Person. With Mom gone, I never want to be fighting with Thorne. It just makes me too sad. So I wash the pots again, sighing big dramatic sighs. Thorne rolls his eyes at me but doesn't criticize my second round of pots. We're always this way with Mom gone, treating each other kind of carefully. But then he flings the dish towel onto the counter and heads toward the back door.

"Where ya going?" I ask.

"Out," he says, teasing me. Probably with Tucker, I think. But I don't ask.

"Take your jacket. It's wicked cold at night," I say. Wicked cold. I like the way that sounds.

With Grandpa snoring away, I head to the cupola. It's so peaceful up here, with the first stars coming out. It's a great place to be sad. I can see the dark shape of Thorne heading through the marsh. I think about Mom and my long-ago dad and all the places I've lived. I let myself sit very still and get a little cold. I'm not sure, but there seems to be smoke rising from the house on Cat Island. A wisp of gray hangs in the twilight. A bat flies by and then another, and I know they are just out catching dinner, but I feel outnumbered by things of the night. Thank goodness, I have a yellow bedroom to sleep in. Thank goodness, I have Old Henry. He wakes me up at night, but I don't care. *"It's too cold for an old man,"* he'll say, and I'll stumble to close the window. He's really terribly bossy, but I don't mind. His brown moon face is so wide and pleasant. Like a cookie. Plus, he never changes. He's the only thing that stays exactly the same. Except for losing that little ceramic fish that used to dangle from his fishing line, he's just the same as when I got him, too long ago to remember. I tried to make him a new fish out of Play-Doh, but he laughed. *"That's okay, princess. I'll just keep fishing."*

At least he didn't criticize my art.

July 2

Mad's not around again, and Thorne's performing endless
cobweb-sweeping at Our Lady. I take my notebook and
hike over to Nowhere Cove. I want to draw Cat Island. I
want to look at Cat Island. For some reason I'm obsessing
about it. I want to tell Mad about the smoke I saw out
there.

By the time I get to Nowhere Cove, I am proud of my
feet. I still don't have any good shoes, so I just go barefoot. I
run my fingers along my soles and they are pleasingly rough
and hard. Not city feet at all. Here in Nowhere Cove, the
insects hum and the redwing blackbirds dive-bomb me if I
go near their nests. I love those birds, so fierce and small.
They don't love me, especially since Oliver has followed me
all the way here. He watches the birds intently, tail switch-
ing back and forth. Occasionally he yawns as if he's not
really interested. (That will be me at whatever school I go to
next: watching intently and pretending I just don't care. I've
got being the new girl down to a science by now, although
it still makes me break out in hives.)

It's too windy to draw, so I start throwing stones. I
stand on the edge of a rock and throw about ten stones,
far, far into the sea. Then I start skipping them. My new

record is fifteen. (My Camp Minnetonka record was a mere eight, and I was considered good even back then!) Mad can't come close. And Thorne, ha!

It's such a muggy day, my skin's all wet. I'm about to jump in, shorts and all, when I hear a cough. It belongs to Grandpa, who is sitting on a rock. It startles me. I didn't think anybody came here except Mad and me. And maybe Mom, long ago.

"There you are," he says, although he must have been watching me for a while. I stare at him. He waves at me with both arms, looking somehow like an old cormorant drying its prehistoric wings.

"Yup," I say, and I make my way over to his rock.

We sit there looking out at Cat Island, and then suddenly Grandpa gets that peculiar expression. His leg twitches, and I can't decide if he's grimacing or grinning or both. It's probably the Icelandic Army again, rescheduling their invasion. I throw another rock as my grandfather answers his foot.

"Emmett Wing," he says, casually, conversationally, as my heart just about stops beating. Because that's my father's name.

"Oh, yes, she's here," says Grandpa, and it's all I can do to stop myself from snatching his leg away from him. As if I could hear anything if I did! I stare at him pleadingly.

"I will tell her." He nods solemnly.

"What? What?" My loud voice perplexes Oliver, who

heads back home to ignore us.

"That was your father," says Grandpa. "He was calling from very far away. Too much static," he sighs. "Too much interference." Grandpa looks me in the eye. "He said to say, 'Hello, Pumpkin.'"

I know Grandpa's crazy, but this feels true. Nobody ever called me Pumpkin except Dad. I stand up and throw ten more stones into the sea, each one farther than the next. Twenty more. Thirty. I throw stones until my arm wants to fall off. They hit the silky sea and drop out of sight, spreading beautiful rings as they go. The rings ripple into nothingness. Erased. Gone.

Hack, hack. Grandpa coughs, and I notice him again. He looks up at me from the rock. I want to ask him everything about Dad, but I know I won't get any answers. I skip another stone out into oblivion. Grandpa starts handing me stones, really good ones. Smooth, flat, skipping stones. Ammunition. I throw them into the sea. My arm is beginning to ache.

Grandpa coughs again, with more purpose. A real throat-clearer. I look at him.

"What I really want is to learn how to swim," he says.

I stop my manic rock-throwing marathon and stare at him.

"But, Grandpa," I say, "you were a sea captain. All those years on the ocean, you MUST have been able to swim?"

"Nope," he says. "Didn't bother learning. The water was always too cold and too fast. If you fell in, two minutes later you'd be drowned. But today it feels a little warmer. Right here. And it's shallow." He looks at me. I look at him, wondering if it's my business to remind him that he's ninety-one years old.

"Can you do it?" he asks. "Teach me to swim?"

I don't really know, but I take this as a dare. "Sure thing, Grandpa," I say. "Sure thing."

July 3

We start the next day. Grandpa has all the wrong instincts. He sinks like lead, and not only that, he's wearing the most old-fashioned bathing suit I have ever seen. He looks like he stepped out of a black-and-white movie. He pulls the elastic waistband high over his belly button. Maybe that's the only way his trunks will stay on. The leg openings flap over his skinny thighs. At least he's dressed. First he told me he couldn't see the point of wearing trunks.

"They'll only get wet anyway."

I told him that the Mademoiselle Aggie School of Swimming required that its pupils be properly attired.

Fortunately, the weather is good for swimming. Grandpa says he hasn't seen a summer this hot in forty-seven years. It's the kind of day when being in the water seems more normal than being out of it. And when the tide is just right, the water is nearly bearable.

"Who says you can't teach an old dog new tricks?" cackles Grandpa, making breaststroke motions in the air as we sit and rest.

In the water he's anything but elegant. Grandpa flails and gasps and swallows half the sea. We start on the dead man's float. First things first.

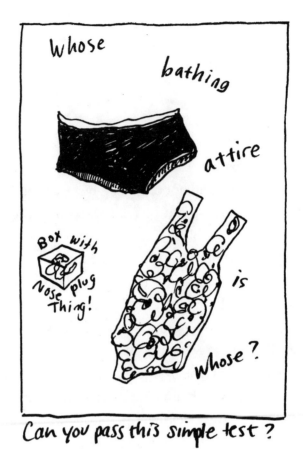

Can you pass this simple test?

July 4

Mad is going out on somebody's boat, and she'll be gone past dark to watch the fireworks in Morning Harbor.

"It's Amy's mom's boat," she explains. "I wish I could invite you."

"So don't I," I say, and we both laugh because that's how Delwyn talks. I tell Mad that it's okay, I'm sure I'll be doing something with Thorne. I want to ask her all about Amy, but that would make Mad think I was jealous or something, which I am.

Mad leaves. Actually, I'm not doing anything with Thorne, because he's not around. Grandpa is taking the world's longest nap. Even Oliver is asleep. I go up to the Quikstop, which is covered in red, white, and blue bunting.

I sit there and mope, drinking more Moxie than necessary. Finally Helen says she's closing.

"There's a parade down to Newington," she says kindly. "Would you like to go with us?"

"That's okay," I say.

I'm so full of self-pity I just want to be alone.

* * *

I am not anybody's darling!

I bring Fig Newtons up to the cupola and sit there looking in the direction I think Morning Harbor is, thinking of Mad, waiting for fireworks.

Finally it gets dark enough.

There are muffled booms in the distance, but it's foggy and I can't see a thing.

Just when I feel the worst, overfull on Fig Newtons

and bored with even Old Henry, I hear the phone ring and take the stairs four at a time.

IT'S MOM!

She says her research is going well. "I'm holed up here at the Love Nest Inn, writing away." I can just imagine her sitting on a motel bed with notes to herself strewn all over the brocade bedspread. Her "literary litter" as Thorne once named it. "This is the perfect place to write a honeymoon mystery," she tells me.

I want to tell her stuff, like about Grandpa and the swimming lessons, how Thorne spends all his time in a church, about Mad, and how I'm really lonely right now but mostly okay, but somehow there's too much to say.

"When are you coming home?" I ask her, noticing that I just called Grandpa's house home.

"Soon," she says.

And that's good enough for now.

July 5

Between the fog ("pea soupers" Grandpa calls them) and
the pine pollen, life in Small Cove is fairly yellow these
days. Mad, of course, is the one who explains about the
pollen. It's this incredibly powdery stuff. You couldn't see
an individual grain with the naked eye if you tried. Just a
cloud of yellow powder. EVERYWHERE. It hangs in the
air and coats all the puddles. Mad says she's seen a tree
release it all at once, like a shout of pollen. I haven't seen
that, but it's a pine tree yelling contest around here, with
yellow icing on everything. Very pretty, but I can't really
breathe.

"Don't worry. The sea breeze will vacuum it up," says
Mad. She's better than any science teacher I've ever had,
and I've had about nineteen of them.

"You'll love Mrs. Hogan at the high school," Mad
informs me, when I tell her this. "She takes us outside and
everything." I get very quiet, glad that Mad thinks I
might stick around for the fall.

"How's the art teacher?" I ask.

"Pretty good," she says, in a preoccupied way. Mad's
painting letters on a boat. She's not really listening to me;
she's concentrating hard. I take the opportunity to talk to
her about Tucker Toothaker, as casually as I possibly can.

I mean, what if my brother is hanging out with a criminal? Anyhow, I like saying his name.

"My own dinghy," smiles Mad, giving the outboard engine a happy slap. She's so pleased to have this boat. It's a seventeen-foot Aquasport, she tells me proudly. She and her dad just came back from carting it up here from Bucksport. She found it through *Uncle Henry's*, this very unfancy newspaper in which you can find *anything* you want. From kittens to canoes. I'm glad it's such a cool paper, because I'm kind of protective of the name Henry.

She's naming it *The Jimmy Carter*, which is what she's painting right now. Mad says she did a project on him and that he's a vastly underrated president. She's painting kind of big, and I can tell she isn't going to get much further than *The Jimmy C.* in bold yellow letters. Yellow, the theme of the week.

Mad is still concentrating hard on the painting, so I ask about Tucker again.

"Tucker?" Mad sighs. "He's okay. I'd like him better if he wasn't in love with his truck."

I'm relieved. At least she didn't say "that jerk!" or "ohmygod!" After all, I leaned against him for almost an hour, even though I didn't mean to. Sort of. And this morning when I saw him out in his boat, he waved at me.

"Cute dog, though," says Mad as an afterthought.

"Cute dog," I agree. "Want to get a Moxie?" (I like Mad, even if she is in love with her boat.)

107

* * *

Tucker does not wear a life jacket, and he stands up in the boat.

(Help! He's so cute.)

I drag Mad up to the Quikstop, feeling guilty. "You can clean your brushes later," I tell her hopefully.

"They'll be ruined," she says cheerfully, then sticks them in a bucket of paint thinner for now. And comes with me.

As we walk we argue about numbers. We can disagree and still be friends. "Don't you think odd numbers are the best? Like seven and three and thirty-nine?"

"Ha!" says Mad. "I completely disagree. Just contemplate the solidity and power of, say, FOUR."

And somehow that's a very satisfying conversation, even if she's dead wrong.

We cross the big road. There's no sign of Thorne by

the church. The grass looks long. I wonder what they're paying him for? There are suddenly a whole bunch of cars whizzing by at top speed. "What's going on?" I ask Mad.

"Summer people," she says in a space alien voice. "They're back."

And I remember Tucker talking about them during our Great Lawn Ornament Mix-up. We went by all these driveways with KEEP OUT signs. You couldn't see the houses, just long, winding dirt roads. No lawn ornaments. "Summer people don't go in for lawn ornaments," Tucker explained to us. "They want their world all perfect and untouched, particularly by us. Don't even want you to look at their ocean."

Having been too busy blushing, I didn't ask him what that meant exactly, so I ask Mad. "Summer people?"

"Yeah. You know, like people from away. From Massachusetts and New York. Like you," she says, laughing, and pokes me in the ribs. "Actually, like me too. I was born in Portland, but that's not enough to make me a real Mainer, since my mom's from Norway and my dad's from Michigan. Like Delwyn says, 'Just 'cause the cat had her kittens in the oven, that don't make 'em biscuits!'"

We swat mosquitoes and count cars. Fourteen in under a minute. That's a lot for a road that cruises through little old Ludwig and ends up in Morning Harbor.

"They come up for the summer, and suddenly the coast is off-limits," says Mad. "I picked blueberries last year and sat right here by the road, selling them to all the summer people. It wasn't bad until that hot day when I fell asleep and woke up with a big, fat guy tapping me on the shoulder, looking down my shirt. I guess I was lucky he didn't just walk off with all the berries." Mad kicks at a stone. "I did make bucks, though."

"Are you going to do it again?" I ask, envisioning a team effort.

"Nah. I might try making some dreamcatchers though. You can sell them for more, and you don't need to kill yourself picking berries."

I think a dreamcatcher business would be really cool. I made one at Camp Minnetonka once. It was a clumsy circle of twigs and feathers. I gave it to Mom, and she said it helped her sleep better, which was a nice thing to say even if it probably wasn't true. Mom must take after Grandpa. She can hardly ever sleep at night. Anyway, I could make a *way* better dreamcatcher now!

We buy the Moxies with some money I have in my pocket. I throw in a couple of Helen's famous whoopie pies. If Mom doesn't get back soon, I'd better start making those dreamcatchers or picking berries. The fifty dollars she gave me is down to fifteen, and I bet Thorne has smoked up most of what she gave him (although he did buy me an Italian the other day). He at least has a job.

Haley Wing, the artist, is sitting at the counter talking with Helen and Del. She looks up at us.

"Hi, girls," she says with a friendly nod.

I gaze at her with way too much yearning.

I'm just dying to tell her that I'm an artist too and that I love her sculptures and isn't it cool that we're both Wings. But all I say is hi.

I can be so pathetic sometimes.

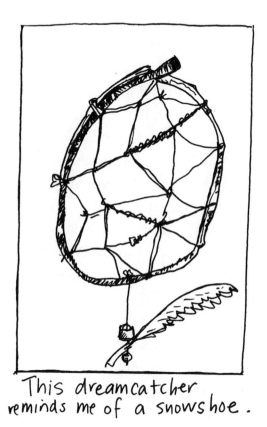

This dreamcatcher
reminds me of a snowshoe.

Mad and I decide to bring the Moxies to Nowhere Cove to try to catch a breeze. It's another sticky humid day.

"Nowhere," I sing in my horrible voice. "Now here." I stretch my arms out wide.

Mad laughs and I feel great.

The tide is out, and the whole world smells like mud-flats, which, in case you don't know, is the smell of sea stuff decaying. It stinks in a nice kind of way. But I could eat one of Helen's whoopie pies anywhere and anyplace. Even nowhere!

We both talk with our mouths full about stars and birds and how there aren't any guys around here except for Tucker and Thorne. Mad goes on about Thorne and asks if he had any girlfriends back in Port Chester. Nope. Although there was a really cool girl in his band. Vera. Then Mad wants to hear all about Vera and Burning Dog, which was the name of Thorne's group. We talk for a long time, and I almost tell her that I have a crush on Tucker, but instead I go quiet and so does Mad. We sit there for a long while as the breeze flaps warm and then cool and then warm again. Like water currents.

"Look," says Mad, pointing to something way out on the flats. "A great blue." We look at it until the whoopie pies are eaten, until the Moxie is gone and is just making us burp. But the heron doesn't move.

"Come on," I say. "That's got to be a post."

"It's a heron, silly," says Mad. She laughs at me. We have this same discussion nearly every day.

"Post!"

"Heron!"

"Post!"

"Heron!"

And we go on like that until the heron finally moves. Because it always is a heron, maybe even the same one. It

The heron in the marsh
just waits
until something good
swims or crawls by.
That would drive me
crazy!

Patience is a virtue?

just looks like a post. I still can't believe something could stand that still for that long.

"Stand quietly on one leg forever, and dinner will swim by," says Old Henry, muffled by my pocket.

And that's a great saying, if you happen to have all day. I'm not great at standing still, personally. I jump up on the rocks behind us. They are the remains of an old stone wall. There used to be more farmland around here, Mad told me. Lots of places were pasture that have gone back to woods, with leftover stone walls in the quietest places. I leap up on the wall, watching carefully for the snake who lives here too. I am happy. I am strong.

I kick a rock. I kick two rocks. I pick one up and throw it to see if I can reach the water, gone way out with the tide.
Almost.
Mad's not into throwing rocks. She's botanizing, bent over some kind of plant.
"Trillium," says Mad. "See how it has three leaves?" She's down on her knees, trying to tell if trillium has any scent.
I pick up another rock. It's jagged and beautiful. I'm going to throw it into the marsh beyond.
At the exact moment I throw it full-force, Mad stands up. Then she falls down again. There is blood, Mad's blood, on the pale white flower. Mad stands up, swaying and stunned, with a thin band of blood trickling down from her temple. I freeze there on the stupid rock wall. Just when I find the words "I'm sorry" coming to my choked-up throat, Mad darts down the path back toward Small Cove and I am left calling her name. The snake pokes its green head out of the wall, and I flinch.

I go running down the path after her, my bare feet jabbed by the rocks. I don't care, let my stupid feet bleed. I run all the way to Mad's house and stand there panting. The kitchen door is shut. I want to go to her, but for some rea-

How to Wreck Your Life in 3 Easy Steps!!

son I can't. This is worse than when I slammed Thorne's finger in the car door and he thought I did it on purpose.

Way worse.

Her mom's car is there. Her mom will wrap her in bandages and give her tea with honey.

What would she do but look at me funny if I came to the door? I am a total and complete idiot. I could give lessons in how to wreck your life in a few easy steps. Illustrated.

I walk slowly up to the church. Maybe Thorne will be there to explain life to me. He's good at that sometimes. A hundred hungry mosquitoes want my blood. I don't even slap them. I don't even run.

The church is locked. Thorne's off somewhere. I peek in at the carvings shining in the peaceful stained-glass light. Maybe there isn't that much to do at the church. It's not like it's a full-time job or anything, although Thorne did tell me that the Reverend Evelyn was due this Sunday. "Big doings," Del said, nodding, when I asked him if she was really coming.

I decide to hide in the cemetery. I sit down next to Grandma's stone. The sound of the stream is so soothing. I imagine my grandma Agatha alive and well and telling me, "Don't worry, honey, everyone accidentally almost kills their best friend at some point or other. It's *normal.*"

I start threading strawberry grass. It gives me something to do while I try to avoid thinking about how to say sorry to Mad. The wild strawberries are sweet and little. They are about the size of a fingernail but taste so much bigger. Maybe Thorne decided this was much too beautiful to mow. I slide the berries off the grass and into my mouth. They taste like summer. They are so perfect that I relax a little. Things will be okay, say the stream and the breeze in the tops of the trees.

I walk around just reading the names. Albert Smith, 1799–1842. That's the oldest one. Bonnie Toothaker, 1943–1991. There are a lot of Toothakers up here. There's little Adeline Swift, beloved daughter. She only got to be two. There are a few *really* old-looking stones with just names and not dates: Mother. Jedediah. Beloved Son. I run my fingers over the letters. Old Henry hops out of my pocket and lands on a little stone by Grandma's. It's smaller and flat. I confess I have been sitting on it when I've come to visit Grandma Agatha because I really didn't know it was a tomb marker. I watch Old Henry walk in the groove of each chiseled letter.

William Thorne Bellicose.

I take a sharp breath and sit down.

William Thorne Bellicose. And not only that, he was born EXACTLY the same day as Mom. He died at age seventeen. This place is too small for there to be any coincidences. Bellicose is just not that common a name.

Did Mom have a twin brother?

"Whoever hunts deer without the forester only loses his way in the forest," says Old Henry, continuing to walk.

He's right. I will have to ask Mom or Grandpa. Thinking about this ties my mind up in knots. The sun beats down on all the mystery and me. I lie back so lost in thought I may as well be dreaming. Clouds blow north like sky sheep, no troubles at all. I am nearly asleep.

"Whatcha up to?" A voice startles me.

It's Mad! She's got a white bandage over her left eye. She's holding a bag of Fig Newtons. "I thought I'd find you here."

I stand up so fast it makes me dizzy, and I give her a big hug. "I'm so sorry," I tell her.

"Course you are!" Mad grins, apparently quite far from dead. "I had to run like that because blood gives me the total creeps." She shrugs. "Not the best trait for a future biologist, I guess. That's why I stick to plants." She gives me a funny smile. "Anyhow, we're even. Remember how Penelope got you the day we met? I've always felt terrible about that."

I smile and feel forgiven.

We sit down in the strawberry grass and eat Fig Newtons. They are a most comforting cookie. Mad eats and I eat and Old Henry stands as still as a heron, but she sees him. "Who's that?"

"That's Old Henry. I keep him in my pocket. I've had him ever since my father left. He's kind of, um . . ." I just don't know how to explain him.

Old Henry bows, almost unnoticeably. He's a very polite man.

"Like a teddy bear?" Mad asks.

"Well, sort of. But not really."

"I've got Nannoo," Mad confesses. "He's still on my bed. He's kind of moth-eaten but I can't throw him out."

I know what she means, although Old Henry is hardly my teddy bear. I belong to him as much as he belongs to me. I pick him up. "He probably shouldn't go in my pocket so much. All that traveling around is getting to him. I think his nose is getting worn off."

"I think he's cool," says Mad, holding him. Old Henry doesn't seem to mind. "He looks like a Chinese gardener."

"Yeah," I agree. "A Chinese gardener near a stream, since he's fishing!"

"With a rock to sit on," Mad adds, all into it. "Hey, let's make him a bonsai world!"

"Cool!" I say, although I can't remember what bonsai is, and there's no sign of Thorne to tell me what it means.

This is what bonsai is: a plant you keep in a little tiny pot so it gets fooled into thinking that the world is very small. That way, enormous pines grow to be merely a foot, or even less. I laugh when Mad tells me this, because it reminds me of ME adapting to the local climate. Like in Port Chester, I used to love pink. But I don't tell her this. If I started to explain my life, it would take forever.

"You have to be careful about watering," says Mad. She is so excited about making Old Henry a home that we get started right away. We find everything we need at Mad's house.

Here's what we have so far—an incredible white dish with blue Chinese calligraphy. Mad's mother gives it to us. She says that the characters spell out a poem. Maybe something about the faraway mountains.

Two rocks. We get these from Nowhere Cove. I don't throw any into the water. Mad doesn't complain that her head hurts. We look at each other and UNDER-STAND.

One tiny bit of moss. Mad feels bad about taking any at all. I tell her that there seems to be enough of it, but she says moss is very picky about where and how it grows. "If you step on it once, it rebounds. If you step on it twice, it suffers. The third time, it will just plain die." I think that this could apply to people too, but I spare her my depressing theories. (I am having too much fun even if my mother is gone, my father is WAY gone, and my brother is impersonating a sexton.)

We dig up a clump of earth with one small maple shoot. "This might really grow," says Mad. And I believe her.

We bring the whole arrangement up to Grandpa's. He's in the kitchen filling a gigantic box full of knick-knacks. "Having a yard sale," he explains. "You could get some money for that," he adds, pointing at the bowl.

We ignore him and go up to the cupola to make Old Henry's Bonsai World. As we walk through the house, it looks different. Stuff is missing. There's no sugar bowl lamp on the landing. There's no painting of flowers by the stairs. I realize that these things are probably what Grandpa has in his box, and then some. I guess it's his stuff, but who'd want to live in an empty house? I check my room on the way by, to make sure he hasn't taken all the books.

"Wow," says Mad when we get to the cupola. "I've always wondered what it would be like to actually be up here."

We spend about an hour making Old Henry's home. My pocket feels a little empty, but Old Henry sure looks great sitting there on his rock, waiting for fish. He winks at me. I wink at him.

Mad is looking out to sea. There's Cat Island. I tell her about the smoke I saw.

"Could have been sea smoke," says Mad. "Or maybe the ghost of Rita Scarp."

I look at her. She looks at me.

"Wanna go there?" she asks.

No matter what, he fishes and smiles.

← a new fish I made

Old Henry

July 6

We go to Cat Island the very next day, after Grandpa's swimming lesson. I have to admit, he's getting pretty good. He can make it all the way from the rocky side of Nowhere Cove to the sandy side. We swim it together. He treads water every few feet when he gets tired. We swim slowly over the swaying seaweed, over the undersea rocks. Eelgrass wraps itself around our arms and necks. I look down when I swim, into the great greenness of the sea, and imagine that I see the shapes of big fish swimming under me. I am the dark shape above them blocking the light.

Then we get out on the shore and shiver and talk. Grandpa takes a phone call. This time it's Honus Wagner, some baseball player who I suspect is long dead. I've never heard of him. Grandpa still gets a lot of phone calls, but never my dad, not since that one time. When I ask him about Dad, he just says, "I think I knew an Emmett Wing quite long ago." When I ask him about William Thorne Bellicose, he mumbles and is interrupted by a phone call. It's someone called Norris about repairing the chainsaw. I can tell I'm not going to learn anything new about family today. Sometimes Grandpa fades out like a radio station.

Sorry— no points for style!

* * *

"Isn't it time for your nap, Grandpa?" I ask, hoping to get going out to the island. After he is settled by the cookstove with Oliver purring madly on his lap, I run over to Mad's.

It's a blustery day, but still hot. I see my silly pink swimsuit dancing on the line I hung between the chicken coop and the back porch. It's probably dry, that's how hot it is. Mad's already in *The Jimmy C.*, and the tide's floating her beside the little dock. It's funny how a boat can be named Jimmy and still be a girl, but that doesn't bother Mad. She's bent over, all red in the face because the engine won't start. She looks up and says it's okay, we'll just row. *The Jimmy C.* has long wooden oars. I've tried rowing, and I can't get the oars to stop popping out of the oarlocks. Mad doesn't have this problem. She pulls in long, even strokes, loosely, easily. The wind blows on us in little oven puffs. Even though it's sweltering, Mad insists that we wear the mildewy orange life jackets that she keeps stowed in the bow. (That's the front. The back is called the stern.)

"Tropical," I say. "And very calm."

"Yup," says Mad. "But the life jacket stays on."

"Jeesum," I complain, like a Mainer.

Cat Island is closer than it looks. After only minutes, we are halfway there. It's just a wooded outcropping of rock, I tell myself. Nothing scary.

"I could swim out to Cat," I remind Mad.

"Don't," says my captain, over the sound of the wind and waves.

And soon we're there. I help her haul *The Jimmy C.* on shore. It's pretty in this little green cove.

Mad gets right down to business. "I'll show you the awful place." We scoot up the hill. There's a small cottage, a shack really, with the roof falling in. I peek inside, but it's dark and spider-webby.

"Did that Rita Cat-Killer person live here?" I asked.

"Nah. She just came out to kill those poor kittens."

I look around. It's a sunny, ghostless day on Cat Island. I don't know why it ever gave me the creeps. Mad leads me to the far side of the island. There by a boulder and some scraggly pines sits a pile of driftwood. It looks like the sea just left it behind, but Mad says she piled it there herself as a monument to all those kittens.

"My brother said he found some kitten bones right here," says Mad, sighing.

"How could she DO such a thing?" we say, hugging each other, frowning. Mad's eyebrows turn into one solid V.

Still, it's very beautiful on this far side. The water is full of silver minnows, like an underwater cloud.

We're so warm that we both want to swim. Mad just starts peeling off her clothes. It's easier for her. Norwegians don't care so much about nudity. I've seen her mom drinking coffee in the sun by their house in just her underwear. When I walked by, she smiled and waved. I can't remember the last time I saw Thorne or my mom with no clothes on, not that I'd want to, for God's sake.

I keep my shorts on. I'm just not that much of a Norwegian. Besides, I have hairs coming in, just a few. It looks like a bald man's head down there, only the hairs are coming not going. Mad's thick with hair, like a grown-up. She sees me staring, but she isn't shy in the least.

"See, this one's Larry and that one's Sue," she says, holding up her breasts. "Larry looks more masculine. See how the nipple is really pointy, like a penis?" We both start laughing so hard that there's nothing to do but dive in.

"I am a mermaid," I say, "and this is Silver Bay." I name the cove for all the minnows that have fled.

"Mud Beach," says Mad in the shallows. She is scooping up handfuls of drippy blue clay. We coat ourselves in mud, the latest summer fashion statement. Mad puts it on me, I put it on her. It feels really gushy, but it dries extremely fast into a new sort of skin. I get some up my nostrils, but it's funny. We walk up on shore, gray ghost girls. We run around shrieking like gulls, giving new names to every place on the little island. The tiny bump of a hill is Lookout Mountain. The tumbledown shack is The Palace. The sad place with driftwood and bones far below is Kittenwood.

We are MudMad and Mudgatha, forever! This is OUR island, our native summer land. Totally out of breath, we lie down on the sharp beach grass with our thick skins protecting us. I notice that there is a wasp on Mad's muddy breast. On Larry. But that is just the sort of thing Mad is calm about.

"So," asks Mad as I stare at the wasp. "Kissed anyone?"

My ears go their usual vermilion. I shrug. I am about to tell her that I ALMOST kissed this guy in Port Chester. His name was Justin, and he was in the cool crowd, the herd. He had crazy, curly hair. But it's not really true. I only wanted to kiss him for a second or two.

"Nope," I say.

Mad is probably about to tell me about her own kissing adventures and what it really feels like to WANT to put your own tongue in somebody's alien mouth, but just then we hear a boat. It sounds really close, so we grab our clothes and run behind The Palace.

"Oh, God," laughs Mad. "It's Tucker Toothaker and the Rideout boys!" We dress faster than fast, pulling our clothes over our dry mud skins. But really, nobody can see us. It's just the two of us, and all at once we are embarrassed enough about that. We clamber over the rocks toward *The Jimmy C.* Mud flakes fly off our arms and legs in the strange, warm breeze. We push *The Jimmy C.* back out into the waves. Mad jumps in like a seal. I roll in like a clown. Then we just bob there on the waves, looking at the island.

"Is it true what they say about your uncle?" Mad asks me out of the blue.

I just look at her, thinking of that stone by Grandma Agatha's. "I don't know," I say. "What do they say?"

Mad hesitates, looking uncomfortable for the first time since I've met her. "Your mom's brother . . . Will. The one who died when he was young, skiing over the ice after his dog. Some people say he made it to Cat Island, but only the dog returned."

I'm looking at Mad, but my mind's running races. So it's true. I think of all the reasons I can that Mom never mentioned a dead brother, but they all stick in my throat like dry toast.

* * *

It's a good thing the tide's going in, carrying *The Jimmy C.* with it, because Mad doesn't row. We just sit there. And she tells me the strangest story. I'm almost sorry that Old Henry is out of my pocket, fishing in his bonsai world. He would have told me, *"Life is stranger than fiction."* I believe that.

It turns out that Mad and I have dead uncles in common. Well, since neither of us were born when they died, they were never our uncles really. But both our moms had brothers, and not only that, they were their twin brothers. That explains my mom's birthdate on the stone.

Mad's was called Björn, and mine was William Thorne. Will.

They *both* died when they were seventeen.

My uncle Will skied over salt ice looking for his dog. Mad's uncle had a much more famous death, at least in Norway. It was in all the papers.

"I'll show you the clipping," says Mad. "It's gone all yellow, and it's in Norwegian, but I know what it says. There's a picture of a sidewalk with a chunk missing. It doesn't look like anything unusual at all, but it was." Björn was hit by a meteorite on his way home from school. It was a tiny rock. Mad says that most meteorites are.

"They aren't falling stars, like I used to think," she sighs, giving the engine cord a few halfhearted yanks. "Most of them burn up before they hit the ground. But this one hit my uncle, and he died."

Two uncles. One chosen by God, the other fooled by his dog.

I've got to go tell Thorne.

We drift closer to the shore. Big clouds are gathering over Small Cove. Dark clouds with thunder maybe. Mad feels the wind shift and starts rowing. We're racing the squall. I hunker down in the new cold wind, shivering and thinking about Will. I turn and look at Cat Island. The trees in our little wood are whipping around like crazy. Fat raindrops pelt the water and fall down my cheeks as if the whole day were crying.

I help Mad pull *The Jimmy C.* way up on shore. We stow the oars and life jackets. We do it so quickly we are like a movie on the wrong speed. Then Mad waves and runs into her house. The rain is really coming down. I run up the hill to Grandpa's, where my pink suit is doing a wet storm dance on the line. I crash breathless into the kitchen, where Grandpa hands me a scratchy wool blanket. I wrap myself up and sit down by the stove like a zombie girl.

"Weather," says Grandpa.

"I was just going to send out the Coast Guard," says Thorne, walking into the room. "Good thing that Mad can row."

I look at them both. The storm isn't on my mind at all. "Grandpa," I ask, looking at Thorne to see how he takes it. "Tell us about our dead uncle, William Thorne Bellicose."

And surprisingly enough, Grandpa does.

"He was your mother's twin, you know. Died when they were hardly grown. Such a fool to think he could catch a dog running on salt ice. He was gone before we could stop him. Never did find his body. Just put a marker up by the church. Your mother went wild and ran away. That's when she left, you know. I'm surprised it took her this long to come back."

Wind and Rain

I refrain from pointing out that she's hardly here. Thorne sits there, numb as a hake, which is what Helen calls people who just don't get it. I bet I look just the same.

When the rain finally turns to mere drizzle, Thorne and I walk up to the church. We kneel there next to the stone marking the short life of William Thorne Bellicose.

"I wonder if he looked like Mom," I say, winding grass around my fingers.

"She's got to come home and stay," says Thorne, in a strange, raw voice. "Otherwise she'll never find what she's looking for."

He's really smart for such a dumb guy.

July 14

If this were a made-for-TV movie, now's when the sound-track would come to a crescendo. I mean, finding out about Mom's brother is pretty big news. But somehow it all just seems to amount to background music with Mom not here to explain. Entire days go by, filled with summer nothingness. I walk around hoping for chickens, raking their little yard. Mad and I make dreamcatchers one morning, in case we go into business. Thorne disappears into the church, into his headphones, into his room. The closest we come to answers is at the Quikstop. Thorne spends a morning there with me, sitting on the spinning stools, listening to Helen and Delwyn talk about Uncle Will and Mom when they were young.

"He had the same red-gold hair she has," sighs Helen.

"They were always together when they were little. Then they got to be teens, and you know, different things got their attention. Your mother had a boyfriend or two, and Will, well, he had his dog. He was the quiet one." Delwyn cuts us each a slice of banana cream pie from inside the glass-domed cake tray. He gives us the pie for free.

"They were both so good with animals," adds Helen, drying coffee mugs.

"Yup," says Delwyn. "Will had a soft spot for 'em. He was always bringing me roadkill, trying to convince me to stuff 'em. That was when he was just a boy. I used to think he'd be the one to take over the taxidermy trade. Right good with his hands, that one."

"And your mother had those chickens," says Helen. "We used to buy some eggs from her. We'd just taken over the Quikstop."

"She was good with them," says Del. "Tamed them, she did. And that's unusual. In fact, that's darn near impossible. Every tame chicken's a masterpiece."

"Ayuh, ayuh," Helen agrees, quite seriously. "A work of art."

Thorne and I just look at each other. It's not only our uncle who's a mystery, it's Mom too. Thorne pulls out his notebook, and we start making a list about Mom. The list we come up with resembles a wacky poem:

Chicken Keeper
Romance Writer
Escape Artist
Sister
Mom
Daughter
Scrabble Queen
Lipstick Lover
Pancake Maker
Insomniac
MISSING!

I miss her.

July 16

Mom the Mystery doesn't call, not even on Grandpa's leg. This is the longest LONGEST LONGEST she has ever been gone.

Thank goodness Grandpa still wants swimming lessons almost every day and Mad still gets me to go off into the woods, or I'd just sit up in the cupola and fret. Thorne's fixing up the cemetery with a little more energy. We even picked some of Mad's mom's lilies and put them on Uncle Will's stone. Grandma's too. Solveig said we could. She said it was a shame that the cemetery is in such bad shape and that she's glad Thorne is here to tend to it.

Somehow the days go by. It's July and the bay is busy with boats. I can see why Maine is called Vacationland, although isn't it a little tacky to put that right on the license plates? Mad and I get back from a long rowing lesson. She's teaching me. I stink at it, but I keep trying. I've even got calluses on the palms of my hands. We're thirsty, so we go up to see if Grandpa has any lemonade. Lately he's been making it from scratch! It beats even a Moxie when you're feeling hot and summery.

But there's no lemonade and no Grandpa. We chug some water and walk back out. And there he is, down past Mad's house, hauling two huge boxes on the old red wheelbarrow. They're his knickknack boxes. They've been sitting in the kitchen for so long I thought he'd forgotten about selling stuff. In fact, the other day, I put one of my favorite paintings back, the one of the winter woods, which Grandpa said was Grandma's favorite. He didn't even notice.

Grandpa seems out of control. His load is bumping like crazy. It looks like he's already lost a lamp and a book out in the grass.

"We'd better help," says Mad, and I agree. We run after Grandpa, hollering "Hey! Hey!" but he doesn't turn around. He's kind of deaf when he wants to be.

By the time we reach him, he's halfway up to the big road. Which is where he's headed. "Time for my annual yard sale," he announces. "Last year I did it in July too."

Mad whispers to me that she doesn't remember Grandpa EVER having a yard sale, but we don't let on. Old people can get pretty set on things. That's what I've learned from living with Grandpa.

We help him push the wheelbarrow up the road. It's hard because the big tire is kind of flat and squishy.

"Perfect," he announces, once he gets up the hill. We're right across from Our Lady and the Quikstop, on our side of the road with the line of mailboxes and the Dumpster. I go check to see if there's a postcard from Mom, but there isn't. For a writer, she isn't much of a writer. In all this time she's only sent one postcard: Niagara Falls—Honeymoon Capital of Canada!

Grandpa takes an old blue cloth out of the wheelbarrow. It looks like it was once something elegant, a tablecloth maybe. I imagine Grandma setting up a nice supper on it, with candlesticks and a soup tureen. Grandpa spreads it on the grass and gravel, right by the side of the road.

"I used to bring a table, back when they let me drive," he explains.

I run over to see if Thorne is in the church so we might borrow a folding table from the basement. There are some down there. Thorne and Tucker were playing poker on one of them the other night and smoking cigarettes. Thorne told me not to worry, because he'd disconnected the smoke detectors, as if that would reassure me any. But Thorne isn't there.

Mad and I help Grandpa set up, although he insists he'd rather do it himself. It turns out he wants to sell everything that reminds him of Grandma, and that is quite a lot.

"Why?" I ask him.

He just keeps unloading the boxes. It's a funny mixture of stuff: antique-looking little figurines of shepherdesses and children, mildewed books and fancy linens mixed in with just plain junk. Who would want a rusty fork?

Delwyn appears on the front step of the Quikstop. He waves and then comes back with one lawn chair and three Moxies. He helps Grandpa into the lawn chair.

"There you are, de-ah," he says to Grandpa.

We sit there drinking Moxies, Grandpa on the chair, Mad and I in the long grass, and nobody stops. What

traffic there is flies by to some other more important des-
tination. The ferry to the Blackberry Islands, maybe.
They're very popular with tourists. Mad says she'll take
me out, but we have to wait until the off-season, when all
the summer people leave.

As much as I don't want Grandpa to sell all of
Grandma's stuff, I start to feel a little miffed on his behalf.
I mean, it's not as if there is NOTHING good here. I'd
buy that lamp, for example, or that old book with the
gold edges. In fact, I want that book.

"Grandpa," I ask, just to humor him. "How much for
that book?"

"Rudyard Kipling?" asks Grandpa. "It's not for sale. It's
yours anyway." And he hands me the book. I sit down in
the shade of the Dumpster and start to read. It's *The Jungle
Books*. Eventually Mad gets bored and says the tide is
right; she's going to do some clamming. The afternoon
gets cooler and buggier, and the book gets better and better. What I love about reading is you can get so far away.

Then somebody stops. It's an old blue station wagon
driven by an even older lady. She opens the door, and I
feel like I should get up and help her out of the car. But I
keep reading, one eye on this person. I've never seen her
at the Quikstop, which is how I define strangers now that
I live here.

The lady has the most washed-out blue eyes. They are
eyes so pale they kind of give me the shivers, like husky

dog eyes. Her face is all wrinkly. A long time ago, I had a ballet teacher named Miss Eleanor. I don't remember much ballet, but I remember she told us that we all get the face we deserve, "so smile, girls." That was her theory: "Smile, smile, smile."

By the looks of her withered-apple face, this old lady has had quite a nasty life. She doesn't even bother to remodel her frown as she comes over. But Grandpa's not afraid, or maybe he's just partially blind.

"Eugene Bellicose," he announces. "See anything you like?"

It turns out that what she wants is to set up next to him. It seems she keeps all her stuff in the back of her car, sort of like a flea-market-to-go. She even has a folding table. Grandpa says he doesn't mind, so they proceed to have a mutual yard sale. It gets later and later, and nobody stops. I go into the Quikstop and get myself an Italian, but Grandpa and the lady don't want anything.

The sun sets, but the yard sale goes on. Only the old woman, whose name is Maggie, wants what Grandpa has, and Grandpa wants what Maggie has, and so they start trading. Helen comes out after closing the store and thinks about buying a teacup, but even when she offers them money, they just keep swapping with each other. And pretty soon it's hard to know whose stuff is whose.

And that's how Grandpa meets his girlfriend, Maggie Carlyle.

Grandpa and Maggie's Yard Sale

July 22

Maggie comes by all week. She wears a wool coat every day, even if it's boiling. I try to ignore the fact that it smells like mothballs. Maybe she keeps a few in her pocket. Maybe she's really 106 years old, and that's what's preserving her. The smell of her drives me up to the cupola (plus, with her around, Grandpa isn't interested in swimming). I try to draw Maggie's face from memory. All those wrinkles are a kind of Braille, as if I'm trying to write her whole life when I draw her face. It keeps coming out wrong. A whole life is hard to draw, I guess. I don't rip up the page, though. I like to look at my mistakes.

"It furthers one to cross the great water," says Old Henry. Sometimes he makes no sense at all. He's a bit like Grandpa that way.

I look across the water. To the left I see Toothaker's Point, and I think about chickens. Out across the bay and to the right is Cat Island. If I look west, up the road, I can see the steeple of Our Lady. All these places have Mom stories to tell. She'd better get back soon. She's got some explaining to do.

July 23

Grandpa and I are doing a jigsaw puzzle. It's a picture of pirate ships. Grandpa likes puzzles with water in them best. Maybe he misses his old life at sea. This seems to be the only time I can get Grandpa to myself with Maggie around all the time now. She's actually talking about putting in a kitchen garden by the back step, even though she doesn't live here. She was pokng around in the dirt as I was fixing up the chicken coop. The coop is looking a lot better these days, thanks to me. (And Thorne thinks HE'S a handyman, ha!) I'm thinking of painting it blue. Since there aren't any chickens, I've been furnishing it with some of the things Grandpa was trying to sell. I don't feel that bad about it. They're kind of like my heirlooms, I figure. Not that I care about stuff like brass fireplace pokers and brocade footstools and antique dishes with cracks. But this is my history we're talking about. So I sequester the soup spoons. (*Sequester* is my new favorite word.)

    We finish the puzzle, something that rarely happens when you only work at night. Grandpa looks up at me, satisfied.

"So," he asks, "are you ready?"

"Sure," I say, just to be amiable. I haven't a clue what he means.

"It's time to get those chickens," he says.

July 24

We row over to Toothaker's Point first thing after break-fast. Who ever heard of getting chickens by boat? But I guess if they flew over the cove in the first place, the ancestral chickens that is. . . . Besides, Maggie won't take us in her car.

"Chicken feathers," she sniffs. Some girlfriend.

Mad lets us borrow *The Jimmy C.* She can't come with us, since she's packing for Audubon Camp. She's going to be away for TWO weeks, a thought that makes me sad and nervous. (What will I do for two weeks? Will Mad still hang out with me when she comes back? Will I still be living here? Mom might come back and move us to Manitoba or someplace else!)

The outboard still isn't working, so that means Mad's trusting me to row. That's a lot of trust. Grandpa refuses to wear a life jacket.

"I can swim, can't I?" he asks. I have a feeling he's never worn a life jacket in his life. Maybe sea captains don't.

I signal to Mad with my oar as we pull out into the waves. She might be gone by the time we return. I pull on the oars and try to remember all the tips Mad told me. Grandpa is sitting in the bow like Goldy, Tucker's dog. He's so light I don't even ask him to move to the stern.

It's pretty windy, but the waves aren't bad, and I'm concentrating so hard on rowing that it seems as if we make it across the cove in no time. The wind brings us a chorus of crowing and clucking. Just how many chickens does Minnie Toothaker keep? She's Tucker's aunt, I found out.

I head for the droopy little dock and hit it with a whack. I have to work on my docking technique. Grandpa jumps out, spry as ever, and secures the boat. I peel off my life jacket, and we walk up to Minnie's.

Minnie's yard is full of stuff. Not lawn ornaments, just useful stuff, or formerly useful stuff. It's like looking at an outdoor attic. Trunks and broken chairs and not-so-broken chairs and snowmobile parts. Several old cars.

AND CHICKENS! There must be forty-five chickens here—it's some kind of chicken convention. No wonder she can part with a few. We walk up to the house. I'm all fluttery with expectation. Finally: chickens!

Minnie's place is part mobile home, part regular, attached in the middle by green plastic siding. There's one scratchy mutt of a dog who ignores us, but I swear, some of these chickens are attack fowl. They come at us, flapping and pecking and squawking. I never realized that chickens could be so fierce! They fly at my face, and I hesitate, but nothing stops Grandpa, who plows through the yard like an Olympic chicken swimmer.

Minnie comes out on the porch, wiping her hands. She's one large lady. There's blood or something on her apron, and it seems she's tilted, but that's probably just on account of her porch being crooked. I don't think I've seen her before, ever. Even up at the Quikstop. Maybe she doesn't get out much.

Minnie stands there, calm as the eye of a chicken hurricane. If I were a really good painter, I would paint her like Van Gogh, with all the lines moving and nothing quiet at all. Agitation, white chickens, green siding, and blue sky.

"This must be Merry's girl," Minnie says, speaking to Grandpa, nodding at me. I nod too. I haven't heard anyone call Mom that since Dad left.

"Yup," says Grandpa. "Aggie, meet Minnie Toothaker." We nod at each other some more.

"Ain't seen your mom since she came back," says Minnie in a grumbly sort of way. I nod again kind of apologetically, not knowing if I should explain that she's hardly back.

"Her dad was Emmett Wing," Minnie says. "He's out west somewheres."

"Ayuh," says Grandpa.

People up here sure know more about me than I do. Even people who stay in their rickety houses and only talk to their chickens.

Minnie is nodding and nodding. I'm doing it too, but I stop. Maybe she has some kind of nervous tic. She keeps wiping her hands and nodding. I try not to stare at her, but she's so fat she makes Helen at the Quikstop look petite.

"How many?" asks Minnie.

"Six," says Grandpa. "And one rooster."

"Sure thing," says Minnie. "I'd just as soon get rid of

Van Gogh would paint the dog green, maybe. He looks so sad.

the little black devil, if we can catch him. He's been pestering Daddy-O some." She glances down at the mutt. I guess that's Daddy-O. Minnie keeps rubbing his ears and consoling him as she speaks. If I were a dog in a chicken yard, I think I might just go crazy. But it's probably worse for the chickens.

"How are they laying?" asks Grandpa.

"Not much," says Minnie. "Most people want 'em for eating." I guess that would explain why she keeps so many and why the chickens are so frantic and fierce. Animals understand everything.

How do you catch a chicken? Forget about it, unless you're Minnie Toothaker. Those chickens flap around us. Pecking chickens, scratching chickens, aloof chickens that fly to trees. Chickens flapping and making droppings. I have to admit that the overall effect is not pretty. I'm not so sure I still even want chickens.

Meanwhile, Grandpa is pointing at chickens as if this is some kind of candy store and he is the kid.

And Minnie, amazingly, is positively zipping around. She's quicker than the crow. She scoops up each chicken and holds it to her enormous bosom. Maybe she is saying good-bye. It occurs to me that she loves these feathered terrorists.

She plops them unceremoniously into a wire cage, like a lobster trap only for chickens. Five chickens, all colors and sizes, and one mean-looking rooster. One more to go.

"Hey," I say, deciding to get into the action. These are, after all, going to be my chickens. "I'd like that one." And I point at the speckled bit of hen by my knee.

"You catch her, you have her," says Minnie, smiling, and I take that as a dare.

I always take a dare.

My mother calls this my character flaw and tells me to use my head, for heaven's sake. Old Henry counsels,

"Modesty in movement." But I can't help myself. Sometimes I just dive into things.

Anyway, that little piece of bird just about flings herself into my arms. "Hello, Ishkabibble!" I say. Which seems to be the perfect name for one remarkably beautiful chicken.

Minnie helps us load the huge, noisy cage into the dinghy. In fact, she hefts the whole darn thing herself. She's strong as well as fast. Grandpa digs into his pocket and pulls out a wad of money and hands it to her. She doesn't even count it, just slips it into her bloody apron pocket and unties the dinghy. Daddy-O stands mournfully at her side, shaking his head as if taking chickens anywhere by boat is too much silliness for one dog to stand.

But there really isn't anyone to see. Thank goodness, no sign of Tucker.

"Thicker than a hull, that Minnie," says Grandpa, as he rows us swiftly home. "And I don't mean her waist size." The chickens cackle nervously in the bottom of the boat. "But she sure can catch a chicken."

The minute we've finished lugging the frantic flock of chickens up the hill by wheelbarrow to their renovated, elegant home, they fly the coop. And it's not like they hike off in one orderly direction. Not at all. It's an explosion of flapping, off into the thistles, behind the house, into thin air. All in the blink of an eye.

I start to feel bad. Maybe they don't like the coop. It isn't very big, but compared to stalking around in broken bits of snowmobiles and lawn chairs, this should seem like luxury! (Not to mention that there's an antique umbrella stand, tarnished silver soup spoons, and a whole bunch of other things in there.) Maybe these chickens don't have a sense of style. Or maybe they're just nervous about their new home. That's a feeling I do understand.

The rooster, whose name shall remain Devil, crows a couple of cocky times right on the fence. Then he too busts out of the joint. Only Ishkabibble doesn't flee. She stays here, right next to me. She must be a chicken of exceptional brain, although that may not be too over-whelming a compliment, by the looks of this crowd.

When I sit down to mope and laugh about the escapees, Ishkabibble hops to my shoulder. Her scratchy feet dig into my skin. It's a good thing she's such a small chicken. Maybe she thinks she's a parrot.

"Damn," says Grandpa, striding off to get his boots so he can chase chickens through the thistles and thorns.

I notice Oliver staring at me through the kitchen win-dow. He's kind of a scaredy-cat, really. I am scratching Ishkabibble's little head. She leans into it like she's been waiting all her life for this tiny bit of attention. Oliver looks away jealously. Then Ishkabibble nips my ear, but not too bad. Her warty little comb flops down over one eye, like a red beret. While I sit there, getting to know Ishkabibble, Grandpa is a marvel of efficiency. Before I can even stand up, he has flung three chickens and one

150

mean rooster all back into the coop. One lands on the brocade footstool, but Grandpa doesn't say a thing.

"This time we close the fence," he says, latching chicken wire to chicken wire.

Maggie comes out of the house and announces grimly, "There's a chicken in the bathtub." Poor Oliver, I think as Grandpa goes in to grab a clucky brown hen. He holds it at arm's length, as if he doesn't quite like chickens. It goes all limp and dead-looking.

Ishkabibble is now perched on my head like a sort of chicken crown: Aggie, Princess of All Chickens. I'm going to be just like Mom, I can already tell—a brilliant tamer of chickens, a poultry EXPERT! Any day now I'll be selling eggs up at the Quikstop.

Grandpa scoops Ishkabibble off my head with absolutely no sense of ceremony and chucks her into the pen. "I'm going in for a nap. *You* find the other one."

I haven't the faintest idea where to look first. I try thinking like a chicken, but I just don't have the experience yet. Maybe chickens have a homing instinct and our lost one is trying to walk home? I stand up and stride purposefully down the drive. Ishkabibble cackles at me mournfully from behind her prison gate. Oliver stares at me from the window. I am the object of multiple reproach, although I swear I can hear Old Henry laughing his deepest belly laugh.

"*Hahahahahahahahahahahahahahaha!*"

Maybe he's laughing because he can see Delwyn, who now comes into view. He's huffing up the hill on his ancient ten-speed bike with our lost chicken tucked under his arm like a squawking football. I could just about kiss the man.

"Thank you!" I say, deftly throwing the returned gray chicken back into the flock, like any old chicken hand would. No problemo. "How'd ya know it was ours?"

Delwyn just smiles. "Just a hunch, that's all."

I smile and wave and realize that now half the town knows about me and my chickens. I spend the rest of the day throwing corn to the flock. My flock.

Introducing: Olivetti (she pecks just like Mom's old typewriter sounded), Greedy (she's the biggest), Indy (who is my second favorite, next to Ishkabibble), Scoot (who is VERY jumpy), Cliché (who is just such a chicken), Devil (the rooster), and Ishkabibble, my own darling Ishkabibble. It's not fair to play favorites, I know, but that's life. Besides, she picked me first.

I introduce Thorne to my chickens. I tell him not to feel bad that they all run away from him. Some people just don't have that chicken knack.

"I can get most of them to take feed out of my hand," I tell him. Well, really just Ishkabibble and Greedy, but I'm working on it.

He raises an eyebrow at me. I don't know why he doesn't find this as entertaining as I do.

"Reverend Evelyn's coming tomorrow," he tells me. "I've got to go sweep." And I figure he's nervous because this is the first time she'll be coming round since

Delwyn returns a chicken.

he's been taking care of the place. I'll bet he has to go downstairs at Our Lady and clean up some poker party messes.

It can't be that he just doesn't like chickens.

July 25

Sunday dawns pinkly and full of cock-a-doodle-doo. Devil seems to think he has to crow before the sun rises and during and after. Mad's still away (I am counting the days!) so I decide I am going to church. Just to see what it's all about. Besides, Mad will want me to tell her about it since it involves Thorne.

Surprisingly, Maggie and Grandpa are coming too. Grandpa's looking spiffy in a striped blue shirt and a jacket. Maggie, of course, is wearing her wool coat. But I can't be critical. I'm wearing a flowered dress that was never supposed to be a miniskirt. I tie a sweater around my waist, thinking it will look more proper up at church.

We inch along the road on account of Maggie's sudden inability to walk. She seems to have dug out her party shoes, and the heels keep sticking in the dirt.

"I'm about ready to get the wheelbarrow and haul you up there," Grandpa says, but he's just teasing. He holds her arm as they walk. Personally, I need my hands free to swat at the mosquitoes. Not that anyone has volunteered to hold hands with me.

Thorne's already up there. He's wearing his beloved hat (I'm beginning to wonder if he still has hair under there), but he's found a shirt with a collar. He can be fastidious about some things. I love that word *fastidious*. It's just so fussy. Words should sound like what they mean. Thorne waves to us from the parking lot. There are about fourteen cars there. "Big doin's," as Delwyn said, no kidding! He's there with Helen. At first I can hardly recognize Helen without her hair net. Delwyn's wearing a suit. Then there are a bunch of other people I recognize from the Quikstop, like the Coffin brothers and some of the other cribbage players and Lacy the Hairdresser. (She offered to do my bangs for free, but I told her I was growing them out. Free gifts make me a little nervous.) And Haley Wing! She's there too. Our Lady of the Wilderness must mean something to her, since she put all those amazing sculptures inside.

I don't see Mad's parents. They're probably out canoeing. I wonder if it shows that this is going to be my second service ever.

We all troop in. Thorne motions me into a doorway. "Want the best seat in the house?"

How can I refuse? Grandpa and Maggie are already settling into one of the pews. It's not like they'll miss me, those lovebirds. I follow my brother up a small winding staircase, to a narrow, airless corridor. It's dark and musty. I sneeze about sixteen times.

"This passage runs right behind the statues," says Thorn proudly. "And you can look out through their eyes."

He's right. I lean close into the whitewashed board and squint through a small opening. I think I am behind the rose-colored moose. I shift to the left and look out through a gilded pine. Down below, everyone is settling.

By now the church is half full, which is probably a big turnout. There are mostly old people here, including three old ladies in matching orange and purple crocheted shawls. They must be the Olson sisters, who live all together down the road. Delwyn delivers their groceries. (Mostly they like lima beans.) There are the bowed heads of quite a few old bald men with sticking-out ears. They're mumbling something. Vague strains of French waft up to us. Grandpa isn't bowing his head. He's just sitting there talking to Maggie, his hand almost on her hand. There are only three little kids, and they're squirming. I don't blame them. It's getting hot, especially up here.

"I'm supposed to sweep everywhere," explains Thorne. "It has to be clean, clean, clean, according to Delwyn. But I figure in a church so full of animals, I ought to let the spiders alone." He pulls a cobweb out of the rafters. It's claustrophobic in this little hall, and his breath is right in my face. It smells like cigarettes. I'm about to ask him if he could possibly be getting paid enough, when a giant loudness rumbles in. Through the eyes of the moose, I see a motorcycle. Everyone is quiet, or maybe just drowned out by the noise. Even the skinny, twitchy kids are motionless, mouths open, their eyes turned toward the door.

"It's the Reverend Evelyn," says Thorne. "It must be."

I refrain from making jokes about the Hell's Angels.

And she rumbles in right through the door! My surprise drowns in the roar of her Harley. "She's the revving Evelyn, you mean," I say to Thorne, who knows I get punny when I'm nervous. Should we really be up here?

Reverend Evelyn
in front of Our Lady

The Reverend Evelyn looks more like a country-western singer, with her long curly hair and snakeskin boots. I giggle, thinking maybe her sermon will be about being left in Kansas by a tall, dark stranger. She's wearing a leather jacket even in this heat. The Reverend is not wearing any helmet. There's a bumper sticker on her saddlebag. I can just make it out: GOD IS MY COPILOT.

I just wish Mom were here to see this. Why *invent* characters?

* * *

At the altar, Reverend Evelyn leaps off her bike. Talk about dramatic entrances. The Reverend motions everyone to stand, and they do. You can practically hear the old bones creaking.

People start to sing. This must be a hymn. I don't know any, but I do love that word: *hymn*. The silent *n* stands for all the unsung hopes. I lean against the wood to hear better. It's somehow familiar to me, especially the chorus. At first nobody's really singing, but the Reverend Evelyn has a good strong voice, and it drags all the other voices out. Sometimes all a person needs is to follow. I almost feel like joining in, but I'm hidden up here like a spy. Grandpa and Maggie are standing up too. Grandpa's looking around, fidgeting a little, another tourist in Churchland. Looking for Thorne and me, maybe.

I'm hot, but the one who is sweating is Thorne. Profusely. And that means a lot! He's leaning over, pressed against the holes for the eyes in the bear, a river sloshing down over his forehead. If only he'd take off the woolen hat, he'd feel a whole lot better. I think maybe we should go back downstairs where it's cooler, but Thorne's looking moderately frantic, imploring me with his eyes, beseeching me even, but I don't want to talk, because now everyone's so quiet, kneeling, bending, sighing, maybe praying.

Thorne keeps sweating. This tiny crawl space is freaking me out. I turn to go back down without him before the narrow passage closes in on me completely.

"Air," I hear Thorne whisper. "Air."

And he pushes open a little door that's level with the heads of the animals. He must know every cranny of this place. I decide to stick my head through a little door too. There are several. Probably Haley had to put them in when she mounted her sculptures up here. We look out over the faithful few, which still amounts to more people than I've seen since I got here. Grandpa is whispering to Maggie. I bet he was one of the bad boys back when he was in school. The air out here isn't really any cooler, just bigger. And bigger helps. I rub some yellow dust off the bear's nose. Pine pollen, I bet. I stifle a sneeze.

Perspiration runs down Thorne's face like rain.

There's a gasp, and eyes flick upward. Thorne and I pull our heads back in, guilty of something we can't name.

Through the eyeholes in the wood, we hear the cry, "It's a miracle! The moose is crying for our sins. I felt it! I felt it!" It's the voice of Avery Neveux, a man I recognize from the Quikstop. He always gets a tuna Italian with two pickles. Thorne and I just stand there panting and sweating in the dark hallway. We can hardly run right down and interrupt the joyous song to say that there was no miracle. Only a hot kid and his sister.

So we sit on the hidden stairs halfway down, feeling neither saintly nor sorry. I start to laugh. Thorne catches it. Let people believe what they will.

Expect a mackerel, that's what I say!

August

August 1

And so it is that the sweat of my brother comes to be responsible for a giant renewal of faith at Our Lady of the Wilderness. The Reverend Evelyn decides to come back the very next weekend. Miracles are good for business, I guess. The Quikstop starts selling a lot more moose magnets, moose-dropping earrings, and moose T-shirts. The next Sunday there are so many people that some cars end up parked over at the Quikstop, and they run right out of Moxies.

August 8

The Sunday after that, it's standing room only. I go to services to make sure Thorne doesn't do any more sweating from above. He doesn't. He just sits in the pew. He seems kind of dazed, like a kid who has set a fire or something. And now he's watching it burn. Everyone's waiting for the next miracle. But why should there be two helpings? Rumors and reports about our supposed miracle have spread all over the place. So much so that the newspapers pick up on it. The Bangor paper runs a short blurb with a picture of the Reverend Evelyn on her motorcycle. The headline reads "Miracle at Ludwig." We're famous from Calais clear down to Belfast. That's what Helen says.

"This is the second time this year Ludwig's made the paper," says Delwyn. "First Emmy Coffin's pig gets out and walks clear to Spit Lake. Now this."

Somehow newspapers outside of Maine get wind of it. Someone even comes up to interview Avery Neveux.

"It's a miracle," he says, right in the *Boston Herald*, "The woods and animals speak. We must listen to them." Maggie says it's a trashy paper and she, personally, would not want to be in it. Still, she buys six copies to send around to all her sister's children.

"Well, I agree about animals needing a voice," says Mad, who came back yesterday, thank God! (And interested in chickens, like any sane person.)

I tell Mad the whole story behind the crying moose. I can't help it. Telling your best friend something doesn't really count as telling. Mad thinks the whole thing is pretty funny, and how do we even know if moose have tear ducts anyhow? "They're not people," she tells me, in that curious voice of hers. "A moose is a moose."

"And a chicken is a chicken," I say, "except when it's Ishkabibble!" And Mad agrees with me that Ishy is just the sweetest chicken alive.

August 10

The dictionary says a miracle is an event that appears unexplainable by the laws of nature; or a person, thing, or event that excites admiring awe. That would be my chickens! Awesome. They seem to have settled into their new lodgings. There's a little bit of chicken poop on the footstool, of course, but I don't have the heart to remove it. Nobody's laid an egg yet, not even my darling Ishkabibble. Delwyn and Helen have stopped teasing me about it, but not Grandpa. He's relentless. The first thing he asks me every morning is if his omelette is available today. But day after day, not a single egg. I keep remembering what Grandpa told me once: that chickens don't lay when they're not happy. I just can't think of what it is I'm doing wrong. I'm dying to ask Mom. I walk circles up in the cupola just itching to talk to her.

"Sometimes it is better to have mysteries than answers," says Old Henry, with whom it is impossible to argue.

Meanwhile, Thorne isn't wasting much time these days thinking about Mom. "Don't worry," he tells me. "She'll be back."

Everything I want to know in Life

I don't know what makes him so sure. Maybe he's got religion or something. Or maybe he's just distracted. The news at the Quikstop is that a film crew might be coming to film Our Lady of the Wilderness Church. Delwyn shakes his head and winks at me, but doesn't take sides. Neither does Helen. They just serve coffee and watch the debate. Was it a miracle or not?

The argument is: Avery Neveux made it all up.

Versus . . .

Avery Neveux experienced the real thing.

"So the moose cried," says Lacy the Hairdresser/Skeptic. "Big deal."

"Can you believe it?"

"Right here in Ludwig."

"Well, there's plenty to cry about."

"Cry in your own coffee."

"I'm having soup, de-ah."

I spin on my stool and feel like an impostor. But it's kind of too late to say anything. And Thorne just wants to let it go.

"So a few more people come to church," he says. "So what?"

His voice doesn't quite convince me, though. I think he just wants to be interviewed by the film crew. Who does he think he is?

The good thing is Thorne's so scared I'll spill the beans that he's bringing me Moxies right and left.

"Thank you," I say. "How about some whoopie pies?"

August 11

Maggie says I have to whitewash the inside walls of the chicken coop or my hens will get some kind of disease. I've heard of whitewash. Isn't that what Tom Sawyer was doing to the fence? She says there's lime in whitewash and chickens need lime and that if I'm not going to whitewash I should just spread lime around. (I don't think she means the fruit!) Maggie also says she wants the chicken droppings to fertilize her garden. So I gather the droppings for her, which isn't the most glamorous aspect of keeping chickens. But at least my hens are producing *something* useful.

I feel like a bad mom. Maggie says to just give them time and not forget to change their water EVERY day. I guess I have a lot to learn. I could use a guidebook to keeping poultry, like the one Mom gave me about hamsters, back in Nebraska when I had Hannibal (he died anyhow). For now I have Maggie and her thousands of opinions.

Still, the flock is getting used to me. And nobody's pulling the feathers off anybody else, thank goodness. But they do have kind of a pecking order. It reminds me a bit of junior high in Port Chester. If you're at the top, you're at the top, and the rooster hangs around with you. Right now Olivetti is in favor. But if it's anything like junior high, that can change in a minute! Greedy, Indy, and Cliché seem to actually care. They peck around the anointed one, hoping some of whatever it is will rub off on them. They strut and preen and pose and do everything but run to the bathroom to apply more eyeliner. Ishkabibble doesn't care about the crowd. She just loves me. And Scoot, well, she's more interested in escape than anything else. I caught her behind the pen yesterday. I have no idea how she got out.

"The fox is gonna get you," I tell her. But I'm not much good at scolding. If I were a chicken, I'd want to be free too.

I'm so wrapped up in my chickens that I forget all about film crews. But they actually come. Thorne runs up to the house like a little kid, beaming. "Hey! They're here!"

And I, adorned with Ishkabibble, smile and say, "They've been here for weeks, fool." But he doesn't mean my chickens.

"It's the national news," he says. "They're going to film Evelyn's special midweek evening worship."

I squint at him. "You're kidding."

But he isn't, so I gently toss Ishkabibble back in with her fellow chicken inmates and walk down to Our Lady of the Wilderness with my brother the miracle maker. I wonder what he's going to do for an encore. If I were Thorne, I'd be nervous, but he doesn't look nervous. He just looks happy. Maybe he thinks Hollywood's next.

I'm about to ask Thorne about this when I feel feathers at my shin.

Isn't this just the cutest chicken EVER?

When she's about to jump onto my shoulder, she does this funny bouncing thing.

Ishkabibble

It's Scoot! Jeesum Crow! I thought I adjusted that gate. Thorne laughs, but he doesn't slow down.

And Scoot keeps following us. Maybe there could be a chicken in the news coverage. That *would* make it more interesting.

*   *   *

Up at the church, the parking lot is overflowing. Cars line the road. It's too dangerous for chickens. I pick Scoot up. She's okay about it.

There are two guys with cameras and all sorts of other strangers running around. Ludwig is a movie set, and we're all extras. I push my bangs out of my face and wish I had a cleaner shirt on. I smell distinctly of chicken coop, but I suppose that isn't really going to show on TV. As if I care! I look around for Mad, but she doesn't seem to be here. She's been working on her boat since she got back from camp, taking apart the outboard like some kind of mechanic. Every time I walk by, I can practically see the thought bubble above her head: "Oh, the adventures we'll have!" And that's just fine with me. She wouldn't be happy up here anyway. She likes it quiet.

There's a platinum blond lady with a cell phone and a clipboard running around yelling things. "Make sure you get the steeple. Take some footage of the old headstones back here. Wait on the store until we get the new sign up."

What new sign? I take a look at the Quikstop as Scoot flaps frantically in my arms. Unbelievably enough, there are two guys on scaffolding, putting up a freshly painted sign: LUDWIG COUNTRY STORE.

Huh?

I'd like to put Scoot down, but I'm afraid she'll get run over. She's really nervous, looking this way and that with her beady dinosaur eyes. Maybe this reminds her of Minnie's chicken yard. Big-time commotion! We duck into the Quikstop, walking right under a ladder, which I try not to do. I tell myself that carrying a flapping chicken cancels out any consequences.

"Delwyn!" I practically yell. "Helen?" The place is so full of people I can hardly move.

"Over here, de-ah," says Helen, steady as a tugboat. I follow in her wake up to the counter. "Quite something, eh?"

She's smiling. She's probably out of Italians by now.

"The s-s-sign," I stutter. "What are they doing?"

"Oh, just a little face-lift, is all." Helen winks at me. "I guess the old one didn't look good enough for them."

I nod, but this makes me mad. How could a new name and stupid lavender paint make this perfect place any better? Anyway, do they want the real thing or the Hollywood version?

"Don't worry," says Delwyn, appearing out of nowhere and patting me on the shoulder. "It's temporary."

Neither of them says anything about Scoot, although I notice strangers looking at me funny. I just wish Scoot were Ishkabibble, that's all. She's a whole lot more cuddly to carry.

Back at the church, I try to find Thorne. He must be inside striking movie-star poses or chatting with Reverend Evelyn. I can see her huge black Harley. It's kind of beautiful, if you like that sort of thing.

Tucker Toothaker is standing right next to it stroking the seat. Goldy's in the back of the truck, which is parked not idling. I guess he's coming to church.

I go over to see Goldy. I'm too shy to just go up to Tucker and ask him about fishing or something. Goldy's tail thumps as I approach the truck bed. "Good girl," I say, scratching her ears. And she is a good dog, because, let's face it, I'm walking around with a live chicken, and she hasn't even growled.

But Scoot does not approve of Goldy. Before you can say "scrambled eggs," she's flapped her way out of my arms and into the noisy crowd.

Aaaaack! I dash after her. I see Tucker laughing at me. He must have been watching.

"Lost somebody?" he asks, but not in a mean way. He's got to be mighty used to chickens, being related to Minnie and all.

"Well, um, yeah." And I'm about to ask him to help me catch her, but just then the Reverend Evelyn and the Clipboard Lady come out of the church. Thorne's right behind them.

"Hey," bellows the Clipboard Lady, who has the right voice for this. "Everyone inside. We're going to get some live footage."

Tucker looks at me and grins, and I can't help but follow him in. Scoot's in the cemetery, where she'll be okay. She'll just have to peck at some graveyard bugs without me for a minute or two.

Inside, everyone is trying to get seated in the long rows of wooden pews, but it's a can of sardines in here. Who *are* all these people? Why have they come?

The cameras are positioned at either side of the altar. It looks like they're rolling already. The camera guys have long hair and expensive running shoes. The cameras are having a strange effect on people. The minute people notice them, they either react like Heidi Rideout, who is fluffing up her hair as if this is an audition for something, or like her brother Tucker, who has gone all quiet and is staring into the stained-glass wood lilies. I'm standing next to both of them here in the back.

Thorne is over by the Reverend Evelyn, talking to a person who seems to be with the camera crew. She's cute and skinny and Asian. Whoever it is, is laughing. Thorne's laughing too and acting like the center of attention, and I wonder what can be going through his head. He started all this. Now what's he supposed to do for an encore? Climb up behind the statues and sweat on everybody again? It just isn't hot enough today.

Can miracles be caught on camera, anyway?

Reverend Evelyn makes a motion. Those people who have a place to sit do so. I'm eyeing the Clipboard Lady, wondering if she'll start barking orders, but she's just frowning and chewing her pen. It's quiet in here now. Too quiet. Everyone's waiting for something. I liked it better when the Reverend Evelyn rode her Harley all the way in. I bet the Clipboard Lady would like that better too, but I'm not directing this Miracle at Ludwig rerun. Anyhow, Reverend Evelyn would run somebody over if she tried that entrance today.

The Reverend starts talking about prophecy and memory and joy, but she doesn't mention any animals or anything I can actually picture, so I get distracted. I keep looking at the camera guys, like everybody else. They're the show, really, not us. I have to stop myself from waving a sarcastic little wave every time a camera turns in my direction. "Hi, Mom!" Yeah, right. Despite the amazing statues, this isn't too newsworthy: a lot of people in one small church at four corners in the woods.

But as we bow our heads for the umpteenth time (ump being a number somewhere out past twenty), there's a rustling and a muffled chicken cackle, and one white feather descends in a dusty, holy beam of light. It lands right on the altar.

"The white heron," says a voice I'm sure belongs to Avery Neveux. "The feather of the white heron!"

Ha. It's Scoot. It just has to be! Thorne's not the only one who can make miracles happen. I edge my way out the door to see how in the world she got upstairs behind the carvings. But meanwhile, the whole church goes crazy. The cameras are rolling as I sneak out the back and up the hidden stairs.

Why is it that nobody notices the obvious?

But I don't find Scoot. Not up in the walkway, not out in the courtyard, not anywhere. I run around like a chicken with its head cut off, a phrase I think I will henceforth avoid out of loyalty to my flock. This is absurd. This is not a miracle! This is just my escape artist of a chicken, out taking a closer look at the world. The service ends, and the crowd flows out of the church. I'll *never* catch Scoot now! I try cornering Thorne to clue him in, but he's all busy with the TV guys. He's deep in conversation with that skinny girl, who up close turns out to be a guy!

"Are you a filmmaker?" I ask him, biting my tongue. I'm afraid I might blurt out the true story of the white heron feather.

"Moi?" says the person. "I'm Cherry." He looks amused that I have elevated him to a professional. I guess he's probably kind of young.

"He's their best boy," laughs Mr. Thorne Know-It-All. "That's someone who helps the gaffer."

I want to ask what a gaffer is, but I don't think I'll give Thorne the satisfaction at this moment. I know I've seen that word in movie credits. *Gaffer.* Someone who gaffs?

"I'm the best boy all right," laughs Cherry, lighting up a cigarette. We walk out into the graveyard near Uncle Will's and Grandma's stones. Our family corner. Thorne lights up too. Smoking is like a language between people, but I'm glad I don't speak it. I stick around despite the stink, since I'm interested in Cherry. He's a breath of city air. He's making us both laugh. Digging Rollerblades out of his backpack, Cherry puts them on, stands up, and tries to skate around on the grass.

"I wear these everywhere, man," he protests, falling over onto Thorne. "Where's the pavement?"

"South," says Thorne.

This is what we learn about Cherry:

His real name is Binh, or something like that, and his family is from Vietnam. He became Cherry his first week in Portland, Maine, long before he started working for the local TV station. He and his brother were busboys at DiTrullo's Floating Cocktail Lounge and Lobster Palace. He fell in love with maraschino cherries and somehow, without realizing it, ate up all six jars in one day and was fired.

"They didn't like me anyway," says Cherry, grinning. "But I got to keep the name."

The filming starts again, so I leave. I've got to find Scoot. This is no place for a chicken.

I trudge down the road, looking under every beach rosebush, calling, "Scoot, Scoot. Here, Scoot." I can hear the crowd up at Our Lady from all the way past the marsh. What's so great about being famous? I wouldn't want my face on TV unless I did something really cool. Something to do with chickens or winning the World Stone Skipping Contest.

Or maybe something to do with art. *The Top-Secret Notebooks of Aggie B. Wing* . . . revealed at last . . . to great acclaim. Hundreds attend opening!

Forget it.

For now I think I will hide in the chicken coop until the film crew packs up and leaves Ludwig. I don't want to spoil anybody's faith in miracles, and I also don't want to lie. And Cherry said that the crew is going to go around Lud-

Cherry

wig and Small Cove and all over the place interviewing people about their experiences at the church and what it's like to live here and everything. And I'm hardly an expert. ("Yes, I have been living here all summer now, and I think blah blah blah.")

I go up to the coop to count heads. The gate is shut. Scoot's still missing. My heart sinks. Ishkabibble clucks over to comfort me. I sit with my chickens for a long while, waiting for one of them to divulge the whereabouts of Scoot. But nobody's talking. Ishkabibble sits on my head, though. She likes it up there. She'd never run off. We're like Mary and her little lamb. One day she'll probably ride the school bus, because now I have to stay here. I can't leave my chickens! And if Mom comes back and insists on leaving again, I'll say we have to take the whole gang with us or I'm not going. Oliver too. Not to mention Grandpa. And most of all, Mad!

I sigh and lift Ishkabibble off my head. I check around the chicken coop for eggs. But there's nothing in there except antiques and chicken droppings. After a while, the smell gets to me and I go in to Grandpa.

Grandpa's having tea with Maggie and Oliver. Oliver's up on the table eating fish from a teacup. I pour myself some strong black tea and add three lumps of sugar, then two more. I just feel I need the energy. Besides, I like the sugar tongs. They're made of silver and look just like chicken feet, no kidding! They're from Maggie's yard sale box. We're just sitting there, warm and lazy, when Grandpa gets that expression. He puts his teacup back on the saucer. It wobbles there as he bends over, ear to foot. Maggie continues to drink her tea, calm as the early morning cove.

"I knew a man who could tell the weather forecast from his toe," she explains, as if Grandpa's phone calls were nothing at all. Just everyday stuff.

"Okeydokey, honey" is all Grandpa says to the person on the other end. He sits up again and takes a sip of tea.

"Your mother"—Grandpa beams at me—"is coming home."

And this is the thing: I believe him.

Old Henry is standing up when I climb to the cupola. The soil in his bowl is awfully dry. I've been forgetting to water. Little maple leaves lie withering all about his world. Mad told me the other day that the ornamental bowl might be a mistake, since it doesn't have a drainage hole. She thought maybe we should just get him an ordinary pot. I hold the watering can high above his head and let it rain, rain, rain. I think maybe he should go back in my pocket. I pick him up, wipe off the rain, and tuck him in. I can't believe I wore these green overalls to a nationally televised church service, but the pockets are good for holding stuff.

"*Home is where the heart is,*" says Old Henry quite happily, his voice muffled and serene.

There's a parade of vehicles and people coming up the drive. One of them is the Channel 52 van. One of them is a Harley. I think about hiding again, but I'm too curious. Besides, if anyone asks me anything, I can always say "no comment."

It turns out that the Quikstop is out of Italians, soft drinks, and pizza makings. They're out of Helen's famous chowder. Basically, they're out of everything. So Thorne

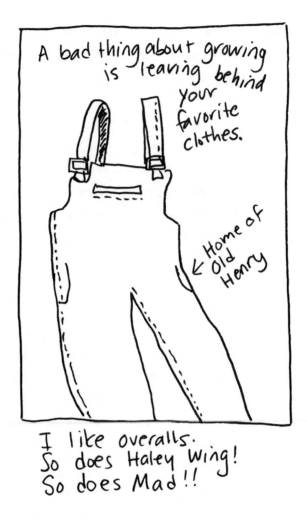

I like overalls.
So does Haley Wing!
So does Mad!!

gets the brilliant idea of inviting the *entire* film crew up to Grandpa's for dinner. Four of them and the Reverend Evelyn too.

Fortunately Grandpa has a big pot of potato-leek soup going and plenty of cans of sardines for sardines on toast. But the film crew is fussy.

"Can't we just get lobster?" asks the Clipboard Lady, so Thorne calls down to the wharf to Rideout Brothers. Tucker answers and agrees to bring up some steamed soft-shells and a bucket of coleslaw. They have a little summer business down there. It's going to be a while, so Grandpa and Maggie settle down to squeezing lemons for lemonade, and the blond lady and the two camera guys walk around filming. It's a perfect Small Cove evening with just enough breeze. The sky is a fine dreamy pink.

My chickens are calling me, so I grab the feed bucket and some compost scraps and head out to the coop. I walk through the little yard and right into the dark, acrid antique shop that is their home. *Acrid* meaning harsh, as in *smell*. Keeping all the stuff rescued from Grandpa's yard sale pile was a better idea before my flock came home to roost. Not that I regret it! I root around among the books and teacups. I open the wooden chess set: no missing pieces. Ishkabibble gives me a friendly little peck on the ear. Still no sign of any eggs. Maybe my mom will know what to do, now that she's coming home. Ishy flies up to my head as I walk out of the coop. I emerge, blinking at the sunset, wearing the latest in outrageous, live head-gear. And of course the Clipboard Lady and a camera guy are standing just outside the chicken wire, filming my flock, filming me. The camera guy is laughing from behind his camera, but the lady's got that serious and sour expression. Truly raw lemon. Maybe she thinks everyone in Small Cove wears chickens. I could be starting a national trend!

I just smile and wave. What else is there to do at this point? I am local color. I am the natives. I am Aggie of Ludwig, Maine. Besides, maybe Isla in Detroit or Leslie in Port Chester will catch me on national TV.

"Hi!" I say, and wave cheerfully. Then I toss Ishy back into the pen and follow the crew up to the house.

"Do you believe in miracles?"

They seem to be conducting some kind of survey. The first and most obvious person to ask is the Reverend Evelyn. They film her sitting on her Harley, looking out to Cat Island. And there's that smoke again, I swear it. Little shivers run down my neck.

"Miracles? Definitely. Daily," says the Reverend in her musical voice. "But faith is what really matters, faith in miracles, not the miracles themselves. They are ordinary." Then she jumps on her Harley and tears off through the salt marsh with a roar. The redwing blackbirds fly up in anger. By the time she reaches the little rise by the big road, she's practically flying.

Then she is gone. (Maybe she doesn't like lobster.)

Our resident crow is cawing his most cantankerous caw, the one that means "Where's the miracle? Your compost is slim pickings today!" (That's because I give the chickens all the good stuff.)

Next up is Maggie, who has come out of the house to hang the dishrags on the line. The slanting rays of setting

Looking at them
looking at us

sun hit her old face. She's grinning a crotchety little grin, mischievous as a five-year-old.

"Miracles?" she says. "If there weren't so many Japanese beetles on my tomatoes, I'd be more inclined—"

"Perfect!" says the blond lady. For her Maggie is just one more sound bite.

"How about you, sir?" she asks Grandpa. He's looking done-in by the lemon squeezing, slumped on a lawn chair that might collapse any minute.

"I'm sorry," he says. "I'm not used to giving parties anymore."

"Miracles," the lady reminds him, using a strange imitation of a gentle, encouraging face. I had a third-grade teacher like that once. We were all afraid of her.

Grandpa clears his throat and spits off into the thistles. He's not too fussy about his national image, I guess. "Well, that depends," he says finally. "With enough wind, chickens can fly over water, and old men can swim to France." His mouth keeps moving a bit, like someone talking in his sleep, but that's all he has to say.

The lady moves on to Delwyn, who has just arrived with Helen, pink from her climb up our hill. I guess they are joining the party.

"Miracles?" says Delwyn, shifting his weight from one foot to the other. He thinks for a while. "Well, I grew a forty-pound zucchini once. That was something." The cameraman laughs, but Delwyn keeps his straight face. I love that man.

Helen is next, but she just waves off the question. "Is there any lemonade, Eugene?" she asks my grandpa. I guess he's famous for it.

Thorne and Cherry are sitting together out by the cliff, enjoying some private joke punctuated by smoke rings.

The blond lady zeroes in on Thorne. "Do you believe in miracles?" she asks him. And I hold my breath. It's the moment of truth.

First he looks appropriately thoughtful. Then he glances at Cherry and kind of grins. "Miracle Whip," he says. "I believe in Miracle Whip."

They both practically fall off the cliff they think it's so funny. The lady doesn't. I'll bet she edits him out.

She turns back toward the house and Cherry calls out, "I do. I believe in miracles." But he isn't from Ludwig, so I guess he doesn't count.

And now it's my turn. I walk over to the chicken coop and fuss with a few things.

"Well . . . um."

The camera guy laughs and stops filming. "I believe in miracles," he says. "Just take a look in that chicken coop. These are chickens of luxury. Fairy-tale chickens. They have their own samovar and what looks to be a Queen Anne chair in fairly good condition." He obviously knows his antiques.

I giggle, hoping he won't blow my cover. The Clipboard Lady rolls her eyes. She thinks he's kidding. The camera eye sees all. The lady just goes on with her script.

I sit down on the edge of the woodpile to compose myself. I'd like to make this answer better than Thorne's. The problem is, I have no idea if I believe in miracles or not. I flip my bangs out of my face, I scratch Ishkabibble, I stare off down the hill.

"I . . . I . . ." Just then I notice something. It's my mother's car, making its way through the marsh. It sure sounds like she needs a new muffler. I spring to my feet and look straight into the camera and smile.

"Yes, I do. I really do." And that's all I have to say.

My mom hasn't even finished parking before I'm hugging her like a deranged lunatic. When she manages to get out of the car, I just hold her. I don't feel like letting her go.

"What's going on up here?" she asks with an award-winning smile. Now *she's* the one who should be on TV. I forgot how beautiful she is.

"It's a long story," I begin, but then Thorne sees her and Grandpa sees her and we're having a little family reunion dance, which, mercifully, Channel 52 neglects to film.

It's getting dark, but there's a calm sea and a pale sky with most of a moon. A gibbous moon, it's called. A waxing gibbous moon, which means it's headed toward full. The bats are out, darting around, eating mosquitoes, but for some reason they don't creep me out. Tucker finally shows up with the food. I notice that my mom knows the right way to eat a lobster. You're not supposed to hack away at it. There's a *system*. She shows me, but I still get squirted, and I'm not quite convinced I want to suck those little legs.

"But that's the best part," says Tucker. "I love legs." He winks, and I blush.

By nine o'clock, Grandpa is asleep in the lawn chair by the backdoor light. Helen and Delwyn are waving and walking home arm in arm. When clouds cross the moon, it's dark.

"Don't worry," says Delwyn, declining the offer of a ride. "We've walked this road a few times."

Everyone else gets into the Channel 52 van except Cherry, who is apparently staying. I'm glad he's here, so I can have Mom all to myself! The time is ripe for her to meet my chickens.

Of course, they're all asleep. All accounted for except Scoot. I shine a flashlight on them, and Mom says, "I'll meet them tomorrow," with a big smile in her voice. We stand there by the coop. I can tell she loves chickens too. As we go in, I think I see lights on Cat Island, looking lonely in the moon-wrinkled sea. I rub my eyes and look again. It's hard to tell what's real or not. I yawn a thousand yawns.

Inside, Grandpa's awake again and working on a puzzle. Mom and I sit down to help him. It's a map of the world. I work on Africa, which is yellow, and Iceland, which is pink, although I refrain from mentioning small Nordic nations by name, since it will just set Grandpa off.

It's hard to talk about what I want to talk about. And Thorne isn't here to help me. He's upstairs with Cherry, listening to German techno-pop *without* the headphones. The drum beats relentlessly on. But I still ask her, I have to ask her.

"Mom, why didn't you ever tell us about your brother?"

Mom stops working on Central Asia and folds her face into her hands. She's not crying, she's just very quiet. She looks up at me after a while.

"I'm sorry," she sniffs. "I don't know."

But the rest remains unsaid.

"He was a nice boy," says Grandpa, finding part of Nepal behind his teacup.

That night I dream of Scoot and all the ways a chicken can vanish into thin air. Grandpa enumerates a few more ways over tea, very early in the morning. Nobody else is up. He thinks he knows the culprit.

"The fox et her," he says, between bites of toast and marmalade. "And that's what she gets for not staying put."

I don't think he should be that judgmental. After all, he got to sail the seven seas. I, personally, suspect Mad's cat, Penelope. Cat of torment and destruction. I saw what she did with that red squirrel she caught last month.

At least we haven't found any sad remains. Wouldn't a dog or a weasel at least leave the feathers? I go upstairs and tear a page out of my notebook and make a LOST CHICKEN sign to put up at the Quikstop. I won't stop searching until I find her, or *forever*, whichever comes first.

Mom appears in the kitchen. After tea, I take her out to meet the gang. Scoot has not returned, but everyone else is up and hungry. Mom greets them all and laughs at their names. She especially likes Olivetti and Ishkabibble, of course (who wouldn't?).

"You're right," she says. "Olivetti's pecking reminds me a lot of me at my old typewriter." We start trying to read Olivetti's chicken poems, scratched out in the dirt.

My mother claims it is a haiku:

Worms are very good,
Tomatoes are very good,
The fox is not good.

We laugh and go up to the Quikstop to post the sign. After that, we go over to the church. It's quiet today, and we just sit by the family gravestones, not saying anything at all.

My poor scoot

August 17

"If somebody tells you it can't be done, stuff cotton in your ears."
Old Henry is exercising in his garden. He moves his
arms so slowly. Sooo . . . slooow . . . ly. He says he's
pushing air. I put him back in my pocket after he's done.
Even though Mom is back now, it feels better when he's
with me. Plus, I think Mad might be right about his pot
not draining. Even the moss looks funny.

Mom says she has to keep writing, she's almost done
with the book, and just to ignore her. It's hard for us to do
that, so she decides to go write in the abandoned trailer,
the one Grandpa's second wife supposedly lived in. I
don't know how she can do that. It stinks in there. But I
guess if you've smoked for as long as she has, you don't
have much of a sense of smell. By her second day back,
she moves down there, pillow and all.

"I love Grandpa's house, darling," she explains to me.
"But it's too hard to stay there. I think of Will. His old
room looks too empty and sad. Even his stuff seems to be
gone." She sighs. "And when I try to sleep, there are
voices in the wall. Besides, I like the little trailer. When I
was about your age, I used to camp out in it all the time.
It was kind of like a clubhouse."

Boys, I think. I bet Mom *never* blushed.

"Back then Grandpa thought he'd take Will and me to see the Grand Canyon in that thing." We laugh. The old trailer looks rooted to the spot.

But even if she isn't going anywhere, I still wish Mom would sleep up here with us.

"When you can't sleep, you could always come downstairs and do puzzles with Grandpa and me," I suggest. She knows. I give her my best dreamcatcher to mount on the trailer wall.

"Thanks, honey," she says. "I love it."

At least she's just down the hill. And I can tell that she's really busy. When my mom is almost done with a book, she spreads the papers all over everything and forgets to eat. When I stopped by with Mad after swimming in Nowhere Cove this morning, she looked up from the floor and said, "Eek! Close the door! There goes chapter three!" All the pages were dancing in the doorway breeze. I had to climb down to the rocks and retrieve page fifty-two: "Sarah's eyes were swollen from crying. Hugo caressed her heaving chest . . ."

I couldn't read any more, but I gave it back to Mom without my usual disapproving frown. After all, she does have loyal readers.

Mom comes up the hill for meals when she remembers to and is *very* useful when it comes to chickens. She says we'll have to put a heater in the coop this fall, which gives me great hope that we might actually be STAYING. I tell

Mad this, and she says, "Of course you are. You're home, aren't you?"

"We're home, we're home," I keep singing through the day, until Thorne tells me to shut up. He's edgy and grumpy. There hasn't been a miracle for over two weeks, and people are losing interest. The Reverend Evelyn has yet to return, and nobody seems to know where she's gone.

"Hollywood is what I heard," says Grandpa.

But that's not who Thorne is missing. I know it. Cherry went back to Portland with the film crew, and Thorne is pining. He has a wretched crop of acne, and his beloved hat is starting to unravel. Even with Mom back, he's a mess. He says he's planning to go down to Portland for a visit, even though Mom says definitely for sure NOT.

The old sign is up at the Quikstop. Tucker and Thorne took the movie prop down for them and put back the old one: Ardis's Quikstop.

"That other one was just too bright," says Delwyn. "Like wearing church clothes on a Tuesday."

"Not to mention it had the wrong name on it," adds Helen.

And even though Ardis is long dead and this is a place where people hang out for hours and hardly ever stop quickly for anything, I totally agree with them.

August 18

Still no eggs. Grandpa is threatening to start eating the chickens.

"Grandpa!" I yell at him. "No!"

I can't really tell if he's kidding or not. We're having a swimming lesson. Actually, we're just swimming. Grandpa has gotten good. Since he and Maggie had some kind of argument a few days ago, he's been practicing a lot.

"What was the argument about, Grandpa?" I ask him. I know he's good enough to talk and swim at the same time, but at first he doesn't answer.

"Can't remember," he finally says, between strokes. The funny thing is, Maggie still comes around to tend her garden. They have tea together, but they just don't talk. It's almost like they're *married* or something!

From the cove we can see the little trailer on the hillside. Mom's in there working away on a beautiful day. Once in a while, she comes out to wave. Well, really to smoke, but she waves too. I float on my back and wriggle my toes at her.

"I love you," she calls down to us.

August 19

Grandpa is missing, totally gone.

"It's not like him to skip dinner," Maggie frets. The hash browns sit untouched. The bowl of chowder has gone very cold. All the butter pools on the top like an oil spill. Even Oliver is walking around in circles.

I check the Quikstop. I check my mother's trailer. I check the woods. I even check the chicken coop. No eggs. No Grandpa.

It's one thing for a chicken to disappear, but a grandpa?

Thorne says he and Tucker will drive up and down the road. Maggie says she'll stay in the kitchen, in case he calls or comes home. As I dash off to go back down to get Mom and make her come with me, Devil is crowing triumphantly. He doesn't like Grandpa much anyhow. Most days he crows right through Grandpa's kitchen nap, until Maggie comes out and swats him with a broom.

I'm breathless when I get down to the trailer.

"This isn't you disappearing," I huff and puff at Mom. "It's Grandpa. It's not *normal.*"

Then I get the most awful hunch. I look out past Nowhere Cove toward Cat Island.

I can't believe it.

I blink.

It must be a seal.

But I would recognize that bad crawl anywhere. It's Grandpa. He's swimming to Cat Island!

That's when I scream.

Mom looks at me.

"A boat," we both say.

We careen down to Mad's house, rocks flying off into the sea below, yelling "Mad! Mad!" but she isn't there.

The Jimmy C. is, and that's all that matters right now.

We leap into the boat. I untie her. Mom yanks frantically at the starter cord, and remarkably, she revs right up. We smack the waves as Mom guns it. Nobody even thinks about life jackets.

We get closer. It's Grandpa, all right, but only the very crown of his bald head. No sailor's cap. His head and hunched shoulders bob up and down on the little waves.

"Grandpa," I holler. "We're coming!" But my voice gets lost in the snarl of the engine, and my heart sinks way into my gut.

Grandpa isn't moving. Not at all.

Once we get close to Grandpa, Mom cuts the motor and we drift alongside him. Grandpa raises his head.

Gasps. Grins. Grimaces.

Then he hangs his arms over the side of *The Jimmy C.* At least he has the strength to do that!

197

"Dead man's float," Grandpa sputters. "Just resting."

I'm holding on to his wet arms for dear life. He looks small in the water, and blue.

"What were you thinking, Grandpa?" I exclaim. We're nose to nose, the boat listing to his side.

"What do you mean, Swim Teacher?" he says, legs still kicking. "I thought you would be proud of me."

And I realize that I am, sort of, since he's alive and everything.

"I was swimming to Cat Island," Grandpa says, bobbing up and down. "Almost made it too!"

"But that's way too far!" Mom wheezes in a strange, strangled version of her voice.

"Besides," I say, scolding him. "You should never swim alone."

But anyhow, he's okay. Still, this is Grandpa after all. He's a geezer of steel.

Getting him into the boat is hard. Very hard. Both Mom and I loop our arms under Grandpa's pale scrawny ones, but then *The Jimmy C.* threatens to capsize. Between attempts, the boat rocks wildly.

"Maybe I'll just swim the rest of the way," says Grandpa, but he's not convincing us. Finally we grab him just right, and Grandpa flops over the side and into the boat. His breath heaves in and out of his bony rib cage.

"I . . . I . . . al . . . m-m-most think the w-w-water is warmer," he stutters, but there's no way we're going to let him slide back in. He's shaking uncontrollably. Mom peels off a layer to cover him, and I take the helm. We're drifting very close to Cat Island. There is a wisp of smoke hanging above the chimney. Somebody's out here.

I look at Mom and gesture with my shoulder. She nods. I know this isn't her favorite place. But where there is smoke, there just has to be a fire to warm up this ice cube of a man. She's holding Grandpa in her arms.

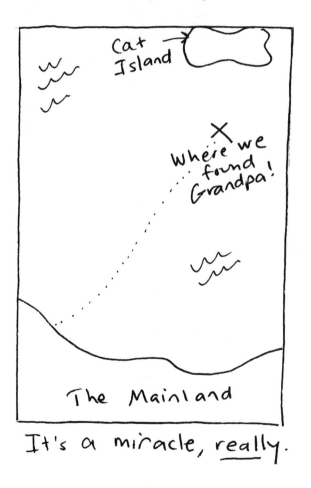

It's a miracle, really.

We're so close I don't bother with the engine. I just row a few strokes, and we hit land.

We come into the cove Mad and I had named Silver Bay that day that now seems so long ago. I jump out and push us in. *The Jimmy C.* slides up on the little rocks. I can see a red kayak pulled up right to the edge of Kittenwood. Mom and I hoist Grandpa to shore. He's very weak but looking mighty pleased with himself. Looking at him smile, you might mistake us for a group of picnickers. Grandpa hangs his dripping arms over our shoulders and walks. Just barely. His feet bump and drag like they're not quite his. We look like we're performing some kind of four-legged race. It's slow going. Out of the corner of my eye, I seem to see a huge carving of a seal, but maybe it's just driftwood.

We stumble to the broken-down door. It's open a crack. All we can hear are gulls shrieking and waves smacking, the usual mournful sounds. Who could be here and tending a fire? Would a doctor with a cell phone be too much to ask for? Just in case Grandpa has hypothermia and is about to die.

"HELLO?" Mom and I call out together.

The door opens wider. Then it falls off its hinges with a *whack*, startling Grandpa's frozen feet into action. Together, we bound into the room, winning the race. There is a burst of chicken in front of our eyes. Of all things!

"Scoot!" I yell, releasing Grandpa to an upended crate. I try to scoop her up but she flaps out the door.

There's a person in the room too. It's Haley Wing! She stands up from next to the smoky fire she's been stoking with driftwood. She looks at us through her funky glasses, her massive braid the color of smoke.

"Here," she says to Grandpa, who is wobbling on the crate. "You look wet, Eugene. Let's get you by the fire."

"Don't mind if I do," says Grandpa, but his legs don't work again, so we have to help him. He lies down on Haley's sleeping bag. He looks up and smiles, then closes his eyes. Grandpa can nap anywhere. I sit there stroking Grandpa's shoulder. I can't help it, I have to lean down and listen to his heart. His rib cage is still heaving in and out. I lie there with my ear on his chest. Hot little tears drip down my face. Somehow, now that it's all over, I'm panicking.

"He was trying to swim here," I tell Haley.

"That's incredible," she says.

"That's Grandpa," I sniff.

Haley offers us tea in shifts out of a shared tin cup. Mom and she haven't seen each other, except for that one day in the Quikstop, for seventeen years or something. Unspoken questions float like icebergs in their chitchat. I watch Scoot from the glassless window. She's strutting up and down along the edge of Kittenwood.

"You seem to know this chicken." Haley grins at me. Chickens are easy to talk about.

I nod. "That's Scoot. She ran away."

"Well, the night before last, the one with all that wind, she ran straight into my cabin. It was too funny. I have no idea how she got here. I figured she was a chicken gone wild."

I nod again. "That's Scoot, all right."

"Maybe I'll make a sculpture of her." Haley smiles at me. "I'm out here working, actually. I sometimes need a new environment. And I'm in this driftwood phase, you see. . . . I remembered this old cabin. A bunch of us used to come here when we were teenagers." She looks at Mom, and they both look sadly at each other for a minute. They are thinking about Will. Nobody talks for a bit. The only sound is Grandpa snoring and the endless swishing waves.

"I miss him too," says Haley after a while. Mom doesn't say anything. She just nods and gazes into the fire.

Grandpa coughs, and we look down at him. He groans in his sleep and opens one eye.

"Do you want to sit up, Grandpa?" I ask.

He grunts and I take that for a yes. Mom and I prop him up.

"Care for some tea?" asks Haley, waving the tin cup.

Grandpa nods. I hold his head as he sniffs and sips as cautiously as a fussy kid.

"I hate chamomile," he insists, but he drinks it all down.

* * *

In a few minutes, Grandpa falls asleep again. We decide that this is a good thing. Haley has stoked the fire so it's roaring hot. Her camp kettle sputters and boils. She and Mom are chatting. It's all about long-ago stuff and people I've never heard of, so I go out to check on Scoot. I sit on the ground as if I don't see her, and she comes over to me.

"No, I don't have any corn," I tell her. "Traitor." But I'm just kidding. Scoot pecks at the ground and flutters her wings. She is a chicken of mystery. How on earth did she get here?

All around us are pieces of driftwood and half-finished sculptures. One definitely is a seal. There's another that looks like a dragon. I look out over the bay. It's getting rough. Little whitecaps run like geese out in the strait between Toothaker's Point and Owl's Ledge. I think maybe we ought to be getting Grandpa home. And us. And Scoot, if she'll go. She keeps strutting over to me then hopping away.

The wind comes up and blows my hair around. The trees in Kittenwood bend and sigh. Scoot's feathers ruffle. She hops indignantly back into the old shack. I follow her inside. Grandpa is sitting up and looking much less drowned.

"I think we'd better go," I say. "There's weather coming."

I peer out the broken door. Every single wave is frothing mad. Weather happens so fast. I tell Mom and Grandpa we just have to leave now. When you're the captain, you must decide. (Sometimes the wind decides everything for you.) Grandpa walks to the boat unassisted. I try one more time to catch Scoot, but she won't let herself be caught. She's just a flash of white in the scrubby pines.

"It's okay," says Haley, putting her strong arm around me. "I'll keep an eye on her. Maybe she'll hitch a ride in with me when I leave."

"You're staying?" I ask incredulously. The clouds just seem so dark and the roof so leaky.

"Yup," says Haley. "Only tonight I think I'll pitch the little pup tent I brought."

I look around at her driftwood sculptures, wishing I were an artist braving a storm with only a wild chicken and the wind for company.

Mom's holding Grandpa, so I try to start the engine. I don't really know what I'm doing. I give it about six yanks, but nothing. By now I've probably flooded it. We wait a minute, then Mom tries. Nothing.

"I can row," I say, talking myself into it. Conditions are getting worse fast, but this seems like the only choice. I make Mom and Grandpa wear the two life jackets, and neither one of them objects. I have become the captain, somehow.

My first stroke doesn't even hit the water. I take a deep breath and try again. Pull through the wave, lift up. Stroke, stroke, stroke. We bob up and down on the rough little waves, and half the time I'm rowing in air. But the

I will lead a brave life.

wind's on our side. We make headway. I'm working so hard I don't think. I only row.

We're nearly there when I hear Tucker's boat coming out to meet us. I don't just know Small Cove by sight, I know it by sound too. And Tucker's boat has the most distinctive thunking engine. I look over my shoulder, and sure enough, it's *The Millicent Marie*. There seems to be all kinds of people on board waving at us. There's also a low, hungry flock of gulls hoping for junk fish following them like a pet cloud. Shrieking. Behind us, a squall has descended on Cat Island and pulled a sheet of rain between us. Cat Island disappears, and I row harder, my heart pounding louder than the waves.

The *Millicent* pulls up alongside us. Mad's on board and Tucker, of course, and Harry Rideout.

"You okay?" shouts Tucker. At least I think that's what he's saying. The wind takes his words away. I nod vigorously and grin at Mad. She grins back. She holds up a line. But I don't *want* a tow. We're almost in, and I want to keep rowing. Sometimes I take after Grandpa, as obstinate as a wild chicken.

The rain's caught us now. I keep pulling at the oars, the shore keeps getting closer, and *The Millicent Marie* just follows us. The gulls have given up. By the time we're all pulled up on shore, rain is dancing on the rocks. Mad leaps out of the lobster boat and onto her little dock. The *Millicent* continues around the point toward the wharf, although she's swallowed up by rain before we see her take the turn.

Then all at once we're all hugging, wet as drowned cats, and Mad's mom comes out to see if Grandpa needs to go to the hospital, since by now everyone from here to Morning Harbor knows he just about swam to Cat Island.

"I'm fine, young lady," insists Grandpa, but I can see that he's ready to be napping in his rocker. Maggie comes running down the hill, her coat straight out behind her like a cape. Grandpa is going to get some scolding any minute now. People get mad when they're sad sometimes.

"Eugene Bellicose!" fumes Maggie. But then she pecks him on the cheek. Mad and her mom both hug me. Mad goes down to *The Jimmy C.* to check things over, and I tag along to help, but I'm shivering and Mad says, "No, I'll see you tomorrow, Captain." And I grin and follow Grandpa and Maggie and Mom up the hill, home.

Nobody says much, but I can tell we're all proud of me. I'm Aggie of Small Cove, to the rescue.

There's not a chicken out in the chicken yard, and who can blame them. In this weather?

When we get in, Oliver rubs himself all over us, purring madly. We're just about to collapse and drink tea when Mom spots a note lying on the wax tablecloth. It's from Thorne.

His cursive is beautiful, but the message makes us all grumble.

> *Went down to Portland for a few days. Visiting Cherry.*
> *Don't Worry. Will call.*
> *P.S. Aggie, can you sweep the church?*

After we finally get Mom back, we lose Grandpa, then we get him back, and now it's Thorne who's gone. I'm beginning to detect a familial tendency. Scoot is just like us, I guess, whether she's here or not.

"Hitchhiking is illegal," my mother says, frowning.

Personally, I'm too tired to go anywhere but to check on my chickens one last time and then on up to bed. I hug Mom, Grandpa, and even Maggie and clunk up the back stairs to my yellow room. I set Old Henry carefully on the windowsill, looking out toward Cat Island, now gone into the night and fog. I think of Scoot out there, and of Haley, but it's not a bad feeling. I make a really quick sketch in my notebook: Cat Island, Suspended in Fog.

"*It furthers one to find the right pillow,*" says Old Henry, just as I drift off.

I have the strangest dream. Like most dreams, it's kind of a patchwork quilt of a movie, episodes sewn to episodes, with no particular rhyme or reason. I wake up with the dream still spinning its wheels, and my head is heavier than the whole world, but since I am remembering it, I write it down. It's still dark. It's very quiet. I don't hear the hiss of Grandpa's kettle, so he's probably not up doing a puzzle.

I am a boulder in a field of grass. Mad comes by and kisses me. She whispers to me that I am a glacial erratic, a piece of a distant mountain deposited at random and far away by the glacier. The glacier is now long gone. I rest in the field. Mad kisses me. I never move again.

Now Delwyn is practicing taxidermy on Scoot, but she's still alive, squawking, flapping, trying to escape.

"Hold still," commands the normally meek Delwyn.

"This must be a Delwyn impostor," I tell myself.

"I have to stuff you and preserve you forever!" he yells, and for a minute I think he means me. But I am not a stone anymore, I am a girl rowing far out to sea.

Then Thorne and Tucker are up at the church, and I am watching from above, peeping out from behind the famed moose. They are rearranging Haley's sculpture and adding in some lawn ornaments: pink flamingos and wishing wells. They are laughing and laughing.

I try to make a picture of the dream, but it's like trying to draw smoke. Then I fall asleep again and sleep like a glacial erratic in a field, rowing its way to the shore. Until morning.

So much depends
upon a far island
  glazed with rain
and featuring
      one chicken....

Cat Island, Suspended
        in Fog

August 20

Devil's crowing; the sun is up. Grandpa, Mom, and Maggie are having tea and arguing about chowder.

"Absolutely no tomato stock," insists Grandpa.

"It's New York style," explains Mom.

"Phooey," says Maggie. "My big, beautiful tomatoes are too good to chop up and cook."

I go out to check on my chickens, and Mom comes too. She's so good around them. They like her a lot, even Cliché, who is nervous and quick. But they still like me best. Arm in arm, we duck into the coop, hens clucking at our heels. There are still no eggs, but Mom says, "Everything in its own time, honey." She says we ought to start bringing some of the antiques back into the house.

"Maybe it's too crowded for them," she suggests.

So we start hauling Grandpa's treasures out of the chicken coop. The books, the teacups, the furniture. It's a huge project involving disgusting chicken poop. I hadn't realized I'd salvaged so much. But Mom doesn't criticize, she just helps me scrape the mess off with a wire brush.

"I remember my mother drinking Darjeeling tea from this cup," she says, holding up the one with the blue roses and smiling.

When she sees the old chess set, she hugs the box to her chest. "This was Will's," she explains. "He was very good at chess." She opens the box and fingers the pieces, but then she puts them away and starts working again.

We move all the stuff out onto the grass. It's quite a pile.

"Just think of all the extra space you'll have, girls," I tell my gang as their beady eyes follow the ottoman, the complete set of James Joyce, the samovar, and the utensils right out the door.

Mom's right. It looks better in there now.

August 21

It's the time of the red, ripe tomatoes around here. Tomatoes fill every bowl; tomatoes line every windowsill. Oliver walks between them with careful cat steps. The crickets chirp all day now, and the Japanese beetles (little metallic bugs that kind of remind me of VWs) are making lace of the rosebush leaves. These things are all signs of the end of summer, says Mad. But that's okay. I'm not going anywhere.

We sit in Maggie's little dooryard garden, fending off chickens. They desperately want to get at the tomatoes. Tomatoes are like chocolate for chickens, says Mom.

Grandpa still has a little cough from his long cold swim. Thorne is still in Portland. He only called once that first night.

"He's only been gone for four days," I tell Mom, but she's still not happy, which is probably exactly how Thorne wants her to feel.

At least she's finished her book. I tell her she should set the next one right here in Small Cove. "It could have two elderly lovebirds in it," I tell her, and she laughs.

She wouldn't have to go very far to do the research.

Grandpa and Maggie are as silly as honeymooners these days. They're making big plans. Big, impossible plans. They want to get on the road with the trailer, the same one Mom's still living in. There are only three wheels on it, but that doesn't seem to bother Grandpa and Maggie.

"Yup," declares Grandpa. "Headed out to beat the winter."

They've been reading travel magazines for a solid week.

"Maybe Florida," suggests Grandpa, who is fond of citrus fruit.

"I already told you. I'd rather be dead than go to that blue-haired place," says Maggie. "Nevada or bust."

"I say Florida. They say the panhandle is mighty interesting," mutters Grandpa, and shuts his eyes to sleep. It's hard to argue with a napping man, although Maggie has a go at it.

"Las Vegas," she insists. "Here we come."

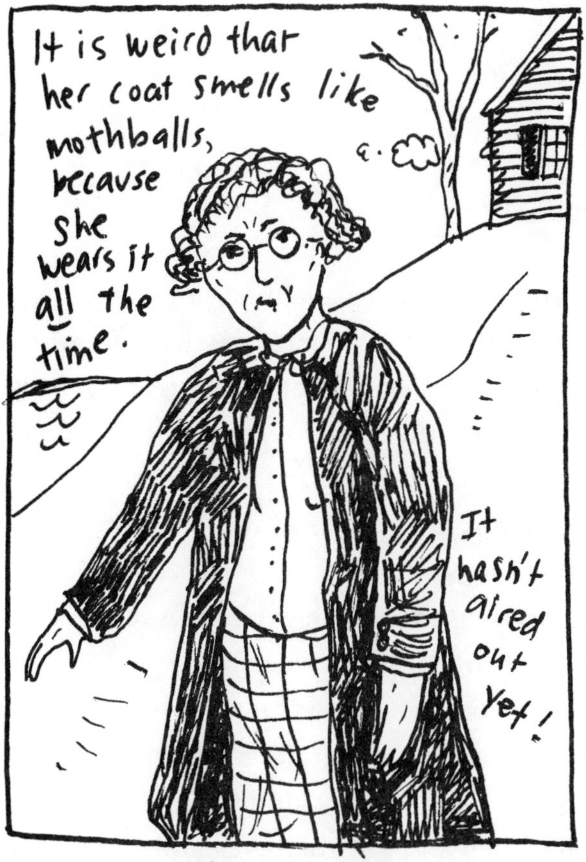

Maggie
(would she wear the same coat in Las Vegas ??)

August 22

Thorne still hasn't called again.

Except last night, on Grandpa's leg! We were eating tuna wiggle, which has Campbell's Cream of Mushroom soup in it (it's *not* the same as Tomato Rice, but still anything by Campbell's makes me pensive). In the middle of a bite, Grandpa got that look and put his foot up by his ear right at the table.

"He's heading to Arkansas, but he says he'll be home soon. He's with that Cherry person."

And this doesn't surprise me. Thorne always said he might try to find Dad. Mom's a bit upset about it. She doesn't think fifteen is any kind of age for cross-country travel. But then she rolls her eyes and laughs nervously and says she bets he's still in Portland.

"Anyway, he has until Friday to come home, and he knows it," says Mom, leaving her plate to go out and smoke by the rosebushes.

August 23

Mom and I go to sweep the church. There's a sign on the door saying NEXT SERVICE WILL BE SEPTEMBER 15. There isn't much to sweep. I guess the action has sort of died down.

"Just the usual customers now," says Delwyn when we go to get the key. "It's nice and peaceful." He winks at us.

Mom and I sweep the church and talk. We go upstairs, and I show her the peepholes where Thorne and I looked out. We laugh about the moose.

"Avery Neveux is an odd duck," says my mother. "When Will and I were little, Avery drove the school bus. We all used to call him Pop. One day he stopped the bus so we could watch the mist rising from the river. He told us all it was elves dancing. Some of the kids made fun of him, but Will and I were only in first grade. We believed right along with him."

It's a clear quiet moment in the church. Mom looks like she's about to cry again. It's about Will, I know. I put my arm around her. Her hair smells like cigarettes. Her eyes crinkle up.

"I told him to go, that day," says my mother, choking on each word. "He was worried about our dog, Shandy. It

217

was mostly his dog, really. I don't even remember why I was angry with him. But with the wind howling and the snow swirling, I got sick of his fretting and pacing and yelled at him 'Just go, then.' And then after a while Shandy came back, but Will never did."

It takes her about four years to say all that. Tears keep falling down her face and onto my arm, but I keep it there, holding her.

"It's not your fault, Mom," I tell her.

She sniffles. "I know," she says, and goes out to smoke in the graveyard. I stay inside, thinking and pretending to dust.

In the slant of light, another small white feather dances down from above. It too lands right on the altar. I hold it in my hand and just know it must be Scoot's.

And it gives me this idea.

"Mom," I say. "We have to go back out to Cat Island."

"Today?" she asks, looking up from the ground beside Will's plain stone.

"Today," I say.

Mad's down by the water mucking around with *The Jimmy C*. The engine's all in pieces again.

"I'm going to get this right," she says, barely looking up.

So we settle for Grandpa's old, leaky boat. It's nameless, but he said I could name it if I want. I'm thinking of *The Agatha Jane*, after Grandma.

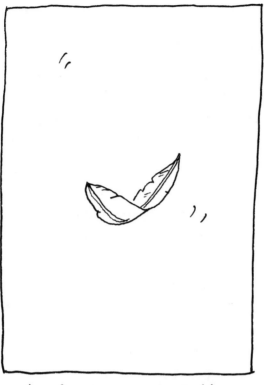

A feather called Hope

I row. Mom bails.

It's a beautiful day. The sun flashes off the water. There's just one little puff of cloud in the sky, like an ad for perfect summer. No wind. A great day for swimming, but that will have to wait. I'm on a mission.

Haley Wing is by the water's edge. Good.

I don't see Scoot. Bad.

Haley waves and helps us drag *The Agatha Jane* up on

the little rocky beach. For a few minutes, we just sit in the sun and soak up the day.

Then I ask my important question.

"Haley, could you help us make a sculpture?"

Mom just looks at me. She doesn't know what I'm talking about. She lights up a cigarette and stares back over the cove.

Haley grins at me, just as I knew she would. "Sure," she says. "What did you have in mind?"

"We'd like to make a sculpture of my uncle Will's dog, Shandy. Sort of a memorial."

"Aha," says Haley.

Mom stubs out the cigarette after only a couple of puffs.

"Out of driftwood," I say. "Or something." Because really I don't know anything about sculpture. We were going to do some in art class in Port Chester, but that's when I left.

"I figure I could draw it out first," I suggest, tracing lines in the pebbly sand with a stick.

"That's a great idea," exclaims Haley.

"Shandy was a big yellow dog," says Mom. "A golden."

And we spend all afternoon on the beach, with Mom talking about Shandy and Will. The little cloud blows out to sea. No wind comes up. We cool our legs in Silver Bay when we get too hot. Haley brings me some paper and a pencil. As Mom talks, I sketch out Shandy. I really base it on Goldy, Tucker's dog, but Mom says it's absolutely perfect and that she looked just like that. "Exactly. You even caught her tongue hanging out and her doggy smile."

Then we comb the island for special wood. I find a piece that looks just like a wagging tail. I run my fingers up and down the old gray branch, wondering where its tree once grew. Far away from here, maybe, like Canada.

Mom finds two beautiful rocks and asks me if I think they could be Shandy's eyes.

"Definitely," I tell her.

Haley brings us wire and small nails and some good advice on joining wood to wood.

We work until we're all way too hungry. Haley says we could stay out here with her, but she has only one sleeping bag and two cans of baked beans. I'm tempted to stay, because it's cool out here with Haley and besides, I haven't seen a flash of Scoot. Haley says she hasn't either, not for two whole days. But then she remembers something and runs into the falling-down shack and comes out with an egg. A perfect brown egg.

"I found this in the little wood," she says, "just this morning."

I hold it for a while. Eggs are such a perfect shape.

Mom smiles at me. "At least someone's laying," she says, laughing.

I hand the egg back to Haley. I tell her she should keep it and boil it up in the teakettle to go with her beans.

"See you tomorrow," I say.

The thing about rowing is you're always facing the place you've just left. To see what's coming up you have to look

How I Picture Shandy
(based on Goldy)

over your shoulder. I point us toward Small Cove and row like crazy. I've really gotten much better at this.

When we're halfway back, I think I see a quick white blur running across the red of Haley's pup tent. I might be imagining things, but I hope it's Scoot.

It's a dangerous world out there. Still, some birds just have to be free.

August 28

All week long, we row out after breakfast and work on our Shandy sculpture. Finally it's perfect. Even Haley says it's really good.

"Emmett would have been proud of you," she says, patting me on the shoulder.

My mother nods. She doesn't even have the funny crease that usually appears between her eyes whenever Dad comes up.

"Who *are* you?" I ask Haley. "My aunt?"

"I wish," smiles Haley. "Cousin," she adds.

And that's good enough for me.

"We should put your sculpture in the church," Haley suggests.

Just like I hoped she would.

Haley says she's staying for a few more nights.

"It's getting cold. Almost September."

Mom just smiles and pats the head of the driftwood dog. We row home with it that very afternoon. It sits proudly in the bow, like a figurehead, guiding us in.

I try not to think about Scoot and how an owl probably got her. Maybe, just maybe, she's flown back to shore.

August 29

Grandpa and Maggie are still around. Big surprise! It turns out that the fourth wheel of the trailer is nowhere to be found. I think maybe Mom hid it because she doesn't think sending a ninety-one-year-old and an octogenarian out on the road is exactly the best idea. She winks at me, but she won't confess.

Fortunately, I can distract Grandpa with eggs. All the chickens are finally laying. Mom says it's because they're happy. They feel at home, she says. So it's eggs every day. Eggs galore! Eggs on toast and over easy. I bring them in, still warm, to Grandpa and Maggie. They immediately start arguing about the best way to cook an omelette. Mom has her own ideas.

"Without onions is best," says Maggie, who always insists on the last word.

August 30

Thorne comes back. He's three days later than he said he'd be. Mom is furious with him but happy. He's alone. No Cherry. Mom and Thorne go outside to have a smoker's duel. That's when two people who should be talking to each other just take great big drags and stare at the horizon, each waiting for the other to start explaining. I follow them out.

"How was Dad?" I ask, because I just can't help it.

"What are you talking about?" Thorne and Mom say at exactly the same time.

Maybe Grandpa wasn't exactly right about Arkansas, but I think in a way he was. Sometimes it's hard to know what you're searching for until you go out and look.

"So how was Portland?" asks Mom, since I've broken the silence.

"Full of brick," Thorne answers, and takes another puff.

I leave them alone and go down to the chickens. Ishkabibble flies to me. I look out over the cliff to Cat Island and beyond. I pull out Old Henry and go into the coop. There by the chicken wire window, I've set his beautiful bowl with the now-dead bonsai. I thought the chickens should at least have ONE treasure. Old Henry settles right down on the rock, all linty and calm. I figure he might want a rest from pockets.

"*In the end, good fortune,*" he says, ducking as Ishkabibble nibbles at the dry brown bonsai maple with obvious delight.

I look through the chicken coop window into the blue square of sky and remember something. It was when I lived in Hawaii. I think I must have been about seven. Dad went parasailing. He drifted like this long-legged

Even if he's gone forever,
I have flown like a bird
with my dad!

speck in the blue. He loved it so much up there in the sky he wanted all of us to go. Mom said NO WAY was she going to get pulled up into the air by a speedboat and dangle from a parachute. And Thorne was pretty cautious when he was a kid. But I said I would do it, and the parasailing people let me, as long as I was strapped right to Dad.

So we flew up together and hung there like a cloud.

Mom and I take Thorne up to Our Lady of the Wilderness. We don't say anything about our Shandy sculpture. But when he unlocks the door and we all walk in, the light is hitting it just perfectly through the stained-glass wood lilies. Shandy is shining gold and green. Purple sunshine dances on her driftwood ears. A rainbow dog sitting there, waiting to play.

"That's beautiful," says Thorne.

And as we stand there, I feel a tiny plop on my cheek. Looking up I see the moose. Thorne watches the giant moose tear running down my neck. He looks up into the wide-open vault. Could it be Mad up there? Maybe pine sap? We both grin because, who knows? Miracles might be for real.

"What's going on, you two?" my mom asks, catching our smiles.

But we just look up and shrug.

"Well, let's get some Moxies," says Mom, and walks out the door. Thorne locks up the church, and we walk hand in hand like second graders over to the Quikstop.

August 31

They're changing the street names around here. Well, that is, they're putting up new signs. The new 9-1-1 Emergency System requires it. I can see how it might be confusing for firefighters who didn't grow up right in Ludwig to find anything. "Turn left after Elsie Michaud's blue mailbox and before the falling-down barn." Yeah, right!

They're letting people name their own streets, so we've been trying to decide what to call ourselves. Mom, Thorne, Grandpa, Maggie, Mad and her family, and me. But the problem is, we can't seem to agree.

"How about Miracle Lane?" says Mad, but I think she's just teasing Thorne.

"How about Mackerel Lane?" says Grandpa, and everybody laughs.

Personally, I think it should be Ishkabibble Drive, but nobody else thinks so.

Then Mad's mom thinks of Rose Hip Lane. Rose hips are those little fruits that grow on beach roses, and there are certainly tons of those on our road. Mad leaps up and picks a big red rose hip for each of us. They look so good I take a huge bite, but it's all seeds. I sputter and spit.

"You have to scrape your teeth along the skin," she explains. "To get the flavor."

So I do, and it turns out that rose hips are sour and sweet at the same time.

"More vitamin C in those than in a whole orange," Maggie informs us.

"No," says Grandpa. "Oranges have more."

"Ounce per ounce, rose hips have more," Maggie insists.

But anyhow, we all agree. Rose Hip Lane is where we live.

It occurs to me that I could get a good pseudonym out of this using the Isla Fire formula: middle name and name of street. I could shorten Bellicose to Belle and use Rosehip.

Belle Rosehip. Ta-da!

But somehow that just doesn't sound like me.

Aggie B. Wing

Artist

Swimmer

Stone Skipper

Rower

Keeper of Chickens

Believer in Miracles

Resident of Small Cove, Maine

Looking at the Forever
Horizon makes me sad
and happy at the same time....

END

of Notebook # 27

(I bought # 28
at the Quikstop!
Where else?)

← I can already tell
it's going to be
FULL of good things....